'Any mo   **ed.**

'One more—   you shut it. Go   ore moving off   in his eyes, and suddenly his arm was round her and his lips were pressing on hers in a long, hard kiss.

She was gasping as she drew back and stared at him. 'What on earth brought that on?'

Piers looked troubled as he gripped the steering-wheel. He said slowly, 'I really don't know.'

Mary Bowring was born in Suffolk, educated in a convent school in Belgium, and joined the WAAF during World War II, when she met her husband. She began to write after the birth of her two children, and published three books about her life as a veterinary surgeon's wife before turning to medical stories.

VERSATILE VET

BY
MARY BOWRING

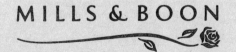
MILLS & BOON

*All the characters in this book have no existence outside the imagina-
tion of the author, and have no relation whatsoever to anyone bearing
the same name or names. They are not even distantly inspired by any
individual known or unknown to the author, and all the incidents are
pure invention.*

*MILLS & BOON, the Rose Device and
LOVE ON CALL are trademarks of the publisher.
Harlequin Mills & Boon Limited,
Eton House, 18-24 Paradise Road, Richmond, Surrey TW9 1SR
This edition published by arrangement with Harlequin Enterprises B.V.*

© Mary Bowring 1995

ISBN 0 263 79097 5

*Set in Times 10 on 12 pt. by
Rowland Phototypesetting Limited
Bury St Edmunds, Suffolk*

03-9507-45824

Made and printed in Great Britain

CHAPTER ONE

THEY were drinking coffee after a long and strenuous morning surgery. Two veterinary nurses and Lindsay Oliver, the twenty-five-year-old veterinary surgeon. At first the talk had been of some of the cases they had just treated but they fell silent at the arrival of Piers Albury, the younger of the two partners. He stood smiling for a moment then pulled out a chair and sat down with a sigh of relief.

'I'm all in,' he said briefly. 'Is there any coffee going?'

Alison, the younger nurse, jumped up willingly.

'I'll get it. Have you had a rough morning?'

He nodded. 'A stallion with colic. Took quite a time and then when at last he recovered the ungrateful beast caught me a swift kick on the ankle.' He paused and laughed. 'I can see from all your sympathetic looks that you're bursting with offers of help but there's no need. The ankle isn't broken and I've rubbed in some stuff that's already working.' He turned as Alison placed a steaming cup in front of him and said, 'You're a ministering angel.'

As he drank, Lindsay was made suddenly aware that his eyes were fixed on her, causing her to wonder what lay behind that searching look. She had come to the practice in the capacity of locum and was a month into her three-month engagement. She had settled in well, liked and was liked by the veterinary nurses, but Piers Albury remained an enigma. When his gaze turned to the other girls, she studied him warily. He was tall, with broad, muscular shoulders, and had thick dark hair and clear hazel eyes under straight black brows. His face was strong and his mouth, in repose, seemed stern but when he smiled his whole face lit up. There was, however, a kind of reserve about him and that reserve intrigued her.

Suddenly she realised that the conversation had turned to the veterinary surgeon she was temporarily replacing. Jessica, the senior nurse, said, 'I had a card from her yesterday. Sydney Bridge, of course. Apparently she loves Australia. She didn't say anything about coming back—still, she's got about six weeks more, hasn't she?'

Piers shook his head slowly.

'She's not coming back. I had a letter from her. The silly girl has got engaged out there and is getting married very soon.'

The nurses gasped but Lindsay was more surprised at the scorn in Piers' voice. Impulsively she said, 'Why do you call her a silly girl? There's nothing silly about getting married.'

Piers put down his coffee and frowned.

'She's stupid to get engaged and even more stupid to get married. And to a businessman who, she says, has a job that entails a good bit of moving around. So the question of her being able to continue practising as a vet is out. A complete waste of her talents and training. I repeat, she's foolish to tie herself down in marriage. Why not just have an affair which would leave her free to break it off when boredom sets in?'

Lindsay stared at him speechlessly and the silence was broken by Alison.

'How cynical can you get? Don't you believe in marriage?'

Piers shook his head. 'No. I think it's outmoded. A trap for two people who, when they want to escape, have to go through all the traumatic business of divorce.'

Lindsay found her voice at last.

'You take it for granted, then, that they will inevitably break up?'

'Yes.' His answer was abrupt and uncompromising. He pushed back his chair. 'Thank you for the coffee.' He began to walk away then stopped. 'Before I go, I'd like a word with you, Lindsay. Will you come into the office, please?'

Shutting the door behind her, he gestured to the chair facing the desk where he seated himself, and sat for a minute in silence while his eyes swept over her in a way that she found embarrassing. She was even more embarrassed when he said unexpectedly, 'What a beautiful girl you are. Gorgeous gold hair, fantastic deep blue eyes and a mouth that is temptation to any normal male.' He grinned as she rose indignantly to her feet. 'Don't go, please. There's no need to get uptight. I have a reason for saying all this.' His mouth twitched at the corner. 'Jumping up like that leads me to one more reflection—what a wonderful figure you have. OK, OK, that's all. Sit down, please. I'm sorry if I've embarrassed you, but you must be used to admiration. Which leads me to the subject I want to discuss. First of all, I must ask you a few personal questions.' He paused. 'How old are you?'

She kept her voice even in spite of her indignation.

'I told you my age when I applied for this job. I'm twenty-five. I graduated last year. I'm doing locums to gain experience before settling down in a practice with a view to eventual partnership.'

He nodded. 'Sensible. Now, are you entangled in any way?'

'Entangled? What on earth——?'

'Well, are you involved in a relationship with a man? Planning to get engaged—thinking of marriage?'

Lindsay's control snapped. 'If you only wanted to discuss my personal life, then you're wasting my time and yours. It has nothing to do with you.'

'Oh, but it has.' He smiled disarmingly, and leant forward in his chair. 'It's like this. The news that Elizabeth is staying in Australia means that we will have to search for someone to take her place. She was destined for a partnership in this practice. You have been doing her work for a month now. With only another two months to go, we must find someone rather quickly.'

Lindsay shrugged. 'You shouldn't have any difficulty. This is a good practice, though, of course, you will have to expand eventually in order to keep up with competition.'

'I'm glad you see that. Jim and I have come to the same conclusion, although Jim—he's sixty-four now—begins to contemplate retirement.' He paused. 'You will see the reason for those personal questions when I tell you that we've decided to ask you if you would care to join this practice permanently with a view—when Jim retires—to partnership.' He stopped as he saw her blink incredulously, then went on smoothly,

'You have proved yourself to be a very good vet. Admirable, in fact. Up to date, yet without the arrogance that sometimes goes with the newly qualified. You're compassionate with your patients and a very good surgeon. Why should we look any further when we have such a good candidate for the position?'

She could hardly believe her ears. Such an opportunity so early on in her career! Surely there was a snag somewhere? She said carefully, 'It's very kind of you and Jim to praise me so highly. The only thing. . .' She paused, gazing at him reflectively. 'Why did you have to ask whether I had any—how did you put it?— entanglement?'

He shrugged impatiently. 'It's obvious, surely? Elizabeth has left us to get married. Your home is down in Devon. I have to know if there is someone there who would take you away from us.'

She raised her eyebrows mockingly. 'What you mean is that if I get "entangled" with anyone, it must be in this area so that I can carry on working in this practice. Is that a condition? Would I have to sign a paper to say that I would content myself with the local talent here in the Thames Valley?'

He burst out laughing. 'How well you put it! Of course we couldn't tie you down like that, but you can't deny that a partnership is, or should be, a long-term agreement, and there is always a lot of trouble if it splits up.' He paused and his eyes swept over her again. 'That's why I was appraising your looks. I don't see you being long without some ardent male wanting to carry you off.'

She drew a long breath. 'You do realise, I hope, that you are being very sexist? Would you lay down the same condition for a male vet?'

He shrugged impatiently. 'Of course not. There's a great difference. A wife usually lives where her husband works. That's why it's so risky taking in a female partner.'

Lindsay frowned. 'I see your point, but I don't much like it.' Suddenly she remembered David. Not exactly an 'entanglement', but on her last visit to her parents in Devon he had talked of getting engaged. He was a chartered surveyor working in a small market town and she had known him for years. She had promised to let him know how she felt about him next time she went home. At last she said, 'I'll think about it. I don't much like the idea of being tied down in my private life.'

'Well, marriage does tie one down, doesn't it?' he said drily. 'That's one of the many reasons I'm against it.'

'Many reasons—what are the others?'

His mouth tightened but he said nothing. Then the silence was broken by a knock on the door and Alison looked in.

'I'm sorry to interrupt, but a client has just come in. Mr Harris—he has a query regarding his dogs.'

'Ah! That's Michael.' Piers turned to Lindsay. 'He breeds gun dogs—English springer spaniels—beautiful animals. Many of them are Field Trial champions. I expect he's got a new litter. He's always done the tail-docking himself—very expertly too—but under this new law it has to be done by a veterinary surgeon, so it will be your job now.'

'Oh, no!' Lindsay looked dismayed. 'That's something I refuse to do. I don't believe in docking dogs' tails. It's unjustified mutilation.'

Piers' eyebrows rose. 'So you're one of the "anti's".
Well, there is a for and against this procedure. But I
don't like the word "mutilation". It's so emotive! I
looked it up in the dictionary. To mutilate is defined
as "to damage or maim especially by depriving of a
limb, essential part, et cetera."' He paused. 'As a dog's
tail is neither a limb nor an essential part, no dog is
maimed by docking. That term cannot be justified in
this context. I don't believe in doing it purely for cosmetic reasons, but for some gun dogs it's a necessity.'
He shrugged. 'We'll discuss this later. If you won't do
the job, then I will.'

He got up and held the door open for her. 'You
must meet him. Mr Harris is an important client.'

He was a big man in his early fifties with thick grey-
ing hair. Introduced to Lindsay, he quickly noticed her
reluctance to do what he wanted.

'The docking must be done tomorrow,' he said. 'The
puppies were born yesterday and I like it done when
they're about three days old.' He hesitated, looking
from one to the other. 'Piers—I rather think——'

Piers nodded. 'Yes, I'll do it. Lindsay is of the school
of thought that doesn't agree with it.'

Michael Harris frowned. 'You call it a "school of
thought"—I call it ignorance. Do you realise that
springer spaniels work in a very different way from
other gun dogs? They don't pick their way carefully
through cover, but crash quickly and forcefully through
the densest hedges. In addition, they have a very rapid
tail action which leaves their tails open to damage.
One of the most difficult injuries to treat is that at the
tip of an undocked tail. Show springer spaniels have

their tails docked by two-thirds, but I consider that quite unnecessary. The working spaniel is only docked by one-third and that, I maintain, saves the dog a lot of misery.'

Piers said, 'Have you got any dogs outside in your car?'

'Yes, half a dozen. I've just come back from Dover, where I went to meet a French client who wanted a six-month-old dog to train. He's made his choice, but he's going to live in Tunisia so the dog must have a rabies injection. I've got the forms and when you've received permission from the Ministry of Agriculture and the injection I'll bring the dog in for you to do the necessary.' He paused, looked at Lindsay, and asked sarcastically, 'I hope you've nothing against injecting against rabies?'

Lindsay flushed and said, 'Of course not.'

Piers, glancing at her quickly, said, 'Let's go outside and see these beautiful dogs.'

Out in the yard, Mr Harris opened the back of his estate car and immediately six springer spaniels crowded against the wire mesh. Tails wagging furiously, limpid eyes full of intelligence, their coats glossy and immaculate, they were irresistible.

'They're gorgeous.' Lindsay stood entranced. 'How could anyone make a choice?'

Mr Harris smiled. 'Well, this Frenchman took a long time. He said he would have liked to buy the lot, but he's already got three. He owns a large estate with a very good shoot and the dogs are looked after like royalty.' He lifted the door of the cage. 'He eventually took this one.' Reaching in, he drew out the chosen one, separating him with difficulty from his eager companions, and let him run around the yard for a few minutes. Then he clapped his hands smartly and immediately the spaniel ran up to his master and sat down. Mr Harris picked him up, held him against his face, patiently enduring the affectionate licking, and proceeded to show off his good points. 'See——' he held out a paw '—he's going to be a big fellow. Look at the size of his feet.' He parted the dog's fur. 'Skin clear and healthy, eyes full of intelligence, and look at his tail. That was docked at three days old. Left alone it would have been two-thirds longer—thick and bushy—and would have caused him great suffering when doing the work he's going to be trained for.' He handed the wriggling dog to Lindsay. 'Not too heavy for you?'

She laughed as she cuddled the ecstatic dog for a few minutes, then, placing him on the ground, she looked up at the two men.

'I see your point about working spaniels, but what about the ones that aren't going to be trained for the gun?'

Mr Harris shrugged. 'I only sell my dogs to the right kind of people. To tell you the truth, I hate to part with them, but one has to live. I always keep some back for Field Trial working.' He turned to Piers. 'I'll expect you tomorrow, then, to do the new litter.'

As he replaced the chosen dog, Lindsay said, 'I see the case for springer spaniels but there are other breeds of sporting dogs—pointers, setters, Labradors, retrievers—whose tails are never docked. Why not?'

'They tend to work on more open ground and have a slower tail action.' Mr Harris looked irritated. 'I suppose you're against shooting, too. You people live in ivory towers, you know.' Then, seeing Lindsay's obvious indignation, he relented and smiled. 'I'll want the new litter injected when it's time. You won't object to that, I'm sure.'

Lindsay laughed. 'Of course they must be injected. I'll look forward to seeing them.'

As he drove away, Lindsay said, 'I'm sorry if I offended him. I can see that he's an important client.'

Piers shrugged. 'He's a man of very strong views and he knows what he's talking about.'

'So do I,' Lindsay said resentfully.

'No, you don't. You used the trendy word "mutilation", yet you take off dew claws, spay bitches and cats without hesitation, knowing that this is all part of your veterinary work. As for docking dogs' tails, I agree entirely with the ban on lay persons doing it. Some breeders are expert, but there are many cases where they do it badly and cause suffering. As a vet you will have to try and ascertain the future lifestyle of a puppy. However, with Michael Harris and his springer spaniels, you know exactly where you are and how necessary the tiny little operation is.'

Lindsay nodded thoughtfully. He was giving her freedom to do as she wished and that was fully in accordance with the advice given by the Veterinary College. She smiled at him.

'Thank you for putting me straight. I'm sure you and Mr Harris are right about his dogs. There are exceptions to every rule.'

'Good girl.' He put his hand lightly on her shoulder and she felt a glow of pleasure at his approval. 'Now, don't forget to let us know as soon as possible about the permanency we're offering you. If you don't want to take it up, then we'll have to advertise.'

She nodded and stood for a moment watching him as he walked towards his car. A strong man, she thought, a man who commanded respect even if one didn't always agree with his opinions.

Still thinking about him, she went in and gave a few instructions to the nurses, then went up to the flat over the surgery which had been allocated to her. Supposedly, if she took up the partners' offer, she would live here permanently. Looking round, she began arranging it to her taste. Then, suddenly, she shook her head. She must think hard before tying herself down. Of course, there would be some time before the actual partnership came up, so, if she changed her mind before that, she could always leave. Cheered by this thought, she went downstairs into the surgery and settled down to some necessary paperwork.

Some time later she answered the telephone and found herself speaking to Piers. In answer to his question, she said, 'No. Nothing booked for this afternoon. See a horse? Yes, I'll meet you there.'

She took down the address and was studying it when the nurses came in. She turned to Jessica.

'Do you know anything about this client? A Mrs Lockwood. I'm meeting Piers at her place after lunch. We're going to look at one of her horses. Here is her phone number so, if necessary, you'll be able to get me there.'

Jessica glanced quickly at Alison and there was such a strange expression on their faces that Lindsay burst out laughing.

'Goodness! What's this all about? Is this Mrs Lockwood an eccentric or what?'

'Well,' Alison grinned, 'do you really want to know or will you tell us off for gossiping about a client?'

Lindsay hesitated, then, seeing their genuine amusement, she smiled. 'I'm getting curiouser and curiouser.'

'Well.' Alison glanced quickly at Jessica, who nodded assent. 'Well, she's the proverbial glamorous, wealthy widow looking for another man and she's making a play for our Piers. At least, that's what we think, judging from the number of times she rings him up, and the way she looks at him when occasionally she comes in to pick up prescriptions. She always wants to know if he'll be here before she comes.'

Lindsay looked puzzled. 'You must be joking. If she's so glamorous and wealthy, why on earth should she be interested in an ordinary vet? After all, we're not exactly noted for the money we make.'

'Ah, but Piers is no ordinary vet. His father has a title which Piers will inherit when his father dies. That's what Mrs Lockwood wants.'

Lindsay gave a disdainful shrug. 'Well, good luck to her.' Then she laughed. 'In view of Piers' view on marriage, I should think she'll have her work cut out. However, the main thing is that I have to meet Piers over there, so I'll leave you two in charge.'

Once more the nurses exchanged meaningful glances and Lindsay frowned. 'Am I imagining things or is there something you're keeping back? Come on, now—what's the mystery?'

Alison shrugged. 'No mystery—just imagination. Piers is obviously out to show her that she's not the only glamorous woman around. As a matter of fact——' she stood back and surveyed Lindsay '—you knock spots off her. She's at least ten years older as well.'

'So that's it!' Lindsay exclaimed indignantly. 'Well, I don't like being used.' She paused. 'I think I'll call it off and pretend someone is coming in so I must stay here.'

'Oh, no!' The girls spoke simultaneously and Jessica added, 'It's only our imagination. Don't take any notice—maybe we're wrong. Do go.' She grinned, 'Then tell us what you think of her.'

Lindsay hesitated, then shrugged resignedly. 'I suppose I ought to. Do you know what's wrong with the horse?'

'Well, Mrs Lockwood has two mares and one of them had a touch of urticaria. Piers treated it successfully and it cleared up, but she's very nervous about it and keeps looking for signs of its return. She's utterly neurotic about all her animals. She's got two dogs and several cats. She pays on the dot, however, and is obviously a good client from that point of view.'

Lindsay sighed. 'We meet all kinds in this profession. Sometimes it's the owners who are in need of treatment rather than the animals.' She paused and laughed. 'I'll try and forget all you've told me so that I have an open mind when I meet Mrs Lockwood.'

She was in a cheerful frame of mind when, after lunch, she went out to her car, and was about to get in when, to her surprise, Piers appeared.

He saw her astonishment and grinned. 'I know. I arranged to meet you at Mrs Lockwood's place, but my last call was in this area so we can go in my car.'

She hesitated. 'I might have to get back—an emergency, perhaps—I don't want to be dependent on you.'

'I'm sure you don't.' He smiled mockingly. 'But I can bring you back at once if necessary.' He held his car door open. 'Come on. Save petrol.' He paused and waited until, rather reluctantly, she got in, Then he added reflectively, 'This is probably an unnecessary call. Sophie—Mrs Lockwood—is a bit nervous where her animals are concerned. I treated one of her mares for urticaria—you know, small areas of skin raised in weals, like nettle rash—probably caused by an allergy to something in her feed. Antihistamines and corticosteroids soon cleared it up, but Sophie is always looking for signs of its return. It could come back, of course— it was mainly over the neck—but the feed has been changed, so I don't think it's likely to recur.'

Subconsciously registering that Piers was on first-name terms with the reputedly glamorous widow, Lindsay said, 'Well, it's nice of you to take me with you, but I can't see that I'll learn much from this visit.'

'It depends. In any case it will be useful for you to get to know Sophie so that if I'm not available you can deal with any problems.'

Lindsay relaxed. Whatever the situation between this client and Piers, it was no concern of hers. Suddenly she was aware that Piers had asked a question and he repeated it impatiently.

'Have you given any thought to our offer of a permanency in the practice?'

'Not much so far. It's all been very sudden. I'll let you know as soon as I decide.'

'Well, don't take too long,' he said, and relapsed into silence.

Soon he turned into a long drive with paddocks on each side. In one of them a solitary mare was grazing at the far end.

'That's Cora, the younger one,' said Piers. 'The other one—Dinah—will have been kept in for my inspection.'

Pulling up outside the imposing front entrance to a large Edwardian house, he got out, saying, 'I'll just find out if she's here or down at the stables. The latter, I expect.'

An elderly woman—obviously the housekeeper—answered his ring and pointed to the left side of the house. In answer to Piers' signal, Lindsay got out and walked with him towards a range of loose boxes. At their approach a slim figure came towards them and Lindsay found, to her amusement, that Mrs Lockwood was almost exactly as she had imagined her: long blonde hair which she flicked back impatiently, a pale, carefully made up face with large blue eyes and a welcoming smile which froze at the sight of Lindsay. Recovering quickly, she spoke directly to Piers.

'I've kept Dinah in. I'm sure I saw a small patch of urticaria on her neck when I looked this morning, but it seems to have disappeared now. I hope I haven't called you out unnecessarily.' She paused, gave Lindsay a cool stare which grew colder as Piers introduced her. 'So you've brought a second opinion. Surely that wasn't necessary?'

'No. Of course not. Miss Oliver is a small-animal vet, but she's interested in horses.'

After a long, appraising stare Mrs Lockwood turned to Piers. 'Well, will you just have a look at Dinah in case I've missed anything? I'll bring her out so that you can go over her thoroughly.'

As the beautiful animal was led out, her coat gleaming in the sunshine, Piers spoke soothingly to her and she nuzzled him in a friendly fashion. After examining her, he smiled rather sardonically.

'All clear. You probably imagined it.' He laughed gently. 'You really mustn't be so anxious. I'm sure, now that you've changed the feed, she won't have a recurrence. However, to put your mind at rest, I'll give her an antibiotic injection to prevent it coming back. I suppose you'll still go on worrying but I assure you it's unnecessary.'

'How well you know me, Piers.' Mrs Lockwood flicked back her hair and gazed at him with such an intimate look in her eyes that Lindsay turned aside in embarrassment. Going up to the mare, now back in her box, she stood stroking the silky head. She was just wishing she had a carrot to give Dinah when she heard Mrs Lockwood say, 'You'll come in for some tea, won't you? I know it's early, but before we have it I'd like you to have a look at my Labrador. She seems a bit off colour. Would you mind giving her the once-over?'

Piers turned towards Lindsay. 'This is your field, Lindsay. Perhaps it would be better if you did the examination.'

'Oh, I don't think so,' Mrs Lockwood said coldly. 'I'd rather you continued to look after my dogs and cats, Piers. After all——' she turned to Lindsay '—it would be a shame to call you from your surgery when Piers is so often out this way. And I can't bear sitting in the waiting-room with all kinds of people.'

Lindsay shrugged indifferently and said, 'I quite understand.' Inwardly relieved, she turned to Piers. 'Don't forget I have to get back for evening surgery.'

Mrs Lockwood frowned. 'Well, there's still time for tea—unless you have any other calls? Naturally you can go back now if you wish.'

Piers said lightly, 'No, she can't. We came in my car. I think tea would be very pleasant.'

Mrs Lockwood's eyes looked cold, then suddenly she said, 'I've changed my mind, Piers—I think I'd like your colleague to examine Goldie after all. Well, just this once anyway.' She turned to Lindsay. 'She's in the kitchen with Mrs Martin, my housekeeper. Piers and I will be in the sitting-room, so would you mind telling her to bring tea in there?'

Avoiding Piers' apologetic look, Lindsay walked quickly ahead, trying to control her anger at this cavalier treatment. The kitchen was easy to find and Mrs Martin looked grimly amused when Lindsay introduced herself.

Taking the dog's temperature, Lindsay looked up and said, 'Normal.'

As she went on with her examination, the house-keeper said, 'There's nothing wrong with her, you know. Still, seeing you've come with Mr Albury, I suppose it was the only way she could get him alone.' Setting out the tea-tray, she added ruefully, 'Silly me! I'm so used to setting for the two of them that I've forgotten a cup for you.' She paused for a moment and gave Lindsay a long, thoughtful look. 'Now we'll have to break up her tête-à-tête with Mr Albury. He's a nice young man, isn't he?'

Lindsay nodded, anxious to get away from this

gossipy woman, whose eyes and voice seemed full of hidden meaning. Following her into the sitting-room, she saw Piers and his client standing by the long window overlooking the immaculate lawns.

Turning, Mrs Lockwood looked coldly at Lindsay.

'Well, what's the matter with Goldie?'

'Nothing at all,' Lindsay smiled. 'She's as fit as a fiddle.'

'Ah! So I suppose you're going to say it's all my imagination, just as Piers does. Really. . .' she paused '. . .you vets! Sometimes I wonder if you know as much as you say you do.'

Stung, Lindsay opened her mouth to retort but Piers forestalled her.

'If you have so little faith in us, Sophie, you shouldn't call us in.'

There was an angry glint in his eyes to which Sophie reacted swiftly.

'Oh, Piers—don't be so cross. You know very well that I need you to reassure me when I get worked up about my animals.' She turned to Lindsay. 'I don't suppose you allow yourself to get sentimental over animals. I expect you get quite hardened. Unfortunately, I'm not like that. I tend to get overwhelmed by nervous fears.' She gave a piteous little smile directed towards Piers. 'You must think I'm a feather-brained creature and I suppose I am. I've always had a man to lean on, you see.'

His mouth twitched. 'Don't think you can make me swallow that, Sophie. I know you too well.'

It seemed to Lindsay as she sipped her tea that something had occurred between them while she had been in the kitchen. Something that had upset Mrs

Lockwood and caused Piers to look grim. The atmosphere was still stiff when at last they said goodbye and Piers was silent for the first half of the journey back. At last Lindsay asked, 'Shall I send in my account to Mrs Lockwood or would you call that examination a—well, a friendly one?'

'Good lord, no! Of course you must charge her. The whole thing was a ruse. She wanted to get me alone. Why on earth did you take so long before you came back from the kitchen?'

'The housekeeper was inclined to gossip,' said Lindsay calmly, then added quickly, 'Is that your bleeper?'

He nodded and, taking the instrument from his inside pocket, he listened, then laughed. 'Well, don't panic. We'll be with you in ten minutes.' Smiling at Lindsay, he said, 'That was Jessica. Apparently someone has brought in an injured bat and the girls haven't the faintest idea what to do about it. How are you on bats?'

'Well——' Lindsay made a face '—I've never had one as a patient. Have you?'

'No, but I've always been interested in them. It won't be easy to treat if it's badly injured. Let's hope the girls put gloves on when handling it. They can bite quite sharply and, although the chances are remote, one must always remember that they can carry rabies. They said they'd put it in a cage, so I expect all is well. Anyway, we shall see.'

Secretly thankful that Piers was obviously going to help her with her strange patient, Lindsay put aside all thoughts of Mrs Lockwood and prepared herself to deal with an interesting case.

CHAPTER TWO

WHEN they arrived at the surgery the bat was in torpor on the floor of the cage and Piers said, 'Good. We can examine it before it rouses.' He turned to the nurses. 'Where was it found?'

'A lady picked it up in the churchyard. Lots of bats there in the evening, apparently. She thought that perhaps a cat had caught it.'

Gloves on, Lindsay opened the cage door, gently drew out the pathetic little creature and looked at it compassionately as it lay in the palm of her hand.

'Pretty, isn't it?' she said. 'Beautiful ears, lovely soft fur—I suppose it weighs about an ounce.' Examining it more closely, she added, 'May I have a magnifying lens, please?' Taking it, she said, 'This makes it easier.' At last she looked up. 'As far as I can make out, the only trouble is this tear in the wing membrane. Of course it may have internal injuries, but we won't know that until it comes out of torpor—if it does.' She paused. 'Piers—what do you think?'

The bat changed hands and Lindsay watched Piers' absorbed expression as his long, gentle fingers examined the tiny creature.

'Yes,' he said. 'I think the tear was probably caused by a cat. Somehow the bat got away before more damage was done. Maybe it bit the cat, which must have given it a bit of a shock.'

'Well——' Lindsay paused '—I'd like you to deal

24

with it, Piers. I'll watch and learn. Will you stitch the tear?'

He nodded. 'There are two ways of treating it. You can use a very fine suture material which is absorbable or a special glue. It should heal quickly and that will allow the bat to be returned to the wild within twenty days.' He paused. 'I think in this case stitching is preferable. It can be done easily while he's still in torpor. Two stitches should be enough.'

He put the bat gently on to the floor of the cage. 'Let's get the material ready. Very fine absorbable suture, please.' He paused again. 'I'm sure there's no need for a general anaesthetic—that's a bit risky.'

Ten minutes later the job was done and the bat replaced in the warm cage. Piers looked round at his audience and grinned. 'Now you've got the task of caring for it.'

Lindsay said thoughtfully, 'There are all kinds of rules and regulations about bats, aren't there? For instance, why did you mention a maximum of twenty days in captivity?'

'Well, on the basis of recent research, it is suggested that after twenty days a bat is no longer a suitable candidate for release. Mind you, that's only a suggestion, but I think it's probably right. As to regulations, all bats are afforded total protection under the Wildlife and Countryside Act. There's also a Bat Conservancy Trust.' He paused. 'In addition, if this bat should die, we have various options as to what to do with the body. The Ministry of Agriculture requires dead bats for screening for rabies and, if poison is suspected, then the Nature Conservancy Council should be contacted. The Zoological Society of London is also keen to receive such specimens. Personally, I think this little fellow will recover and live to go back to the place where he was found.'

'What do we do about feeding, and how often?'

'Well, water in a shallow container must always be provided and, for eating, I think tinned cat food will do the trick. You could add cottage cheese for the calcium content, but the bat mustn't get so fat that it can't climb the cage wall and has to roost on the floor. We'll have to see how it goes.'

'But if it doesn't make any progress,' Lindsay asked, 'should it be euthanised?'

'I don't think it will come to that but if it does deteriorate, then that would be the kindest course.'

Piers was silent as he gazed at the little captive then he said,

'Those wings are huge in comparison with the small body. They open about fourteen inches, you know. When it takes anything to eat, it brings it round in front of its mouth, hiding its head the way birds of prey do when they feed.'

Suddenly Alison, who had been silent for a long time, said, 'Well, you can say what you like but it gives me the horrors. It's so weird—so—so Dracula-like.' She giggled. 'Of course, that's what we'll call it—Dracula.'

Piers burst out laughing. 'That's a bit hard. It's not a vampire bat. Still, I can see you've made up your mind. Dracula it will have to be.'

After a busy evening surgery, Lindsay went to study the bat's progress. He was beginning to move around slowly and she was pleased to see that he had taken some of the warmed milk which was in a saucer on the floor of his cage. Satisfied, she was about to turn away when Piers came in and stood beside her. He said, 'If he continues to drink, we'll put a fluid anti-biotic into the saucer to prevent infection. He's doing well so far.'

He was on the point of going out of the room when Lindsay said impulsively, 'I've made up my mind about your offer. Would you like to hear my decision now?'

He turned swiftly. 'I'd rather discuss it later. How about coming to my house this evening? Jim is coming round for a drink. If your answer is no, then perhaps the two of us can persuade you to change your mind, and if it's yes, then we can get down to details. How about eight-thirty?'

It seemed a good idea and punctually that evening Lindsay drove into the driveway of his house and found him waiting for her. He said, 'Jim won't be here till nine o'clock. It's such a lovely evening, so how about coming round the garden?'

Suddenly a large dog came bounding towards them and she laughed as she bent to pat him. 'What exactly is he? A collie cross?'

Piers grinned. 'You may well ask. He's a bit of collie, but the rest is a mystery. I rescued him from a bad home—paid well over the odds, too—and luckily he's responded to kindness. We're great friends.' Bending down, he said, 'Shake hands with Lindsay.'

There was a moment's hesitation as he studied his master's visitor, then a large, shaggy paw was slowly lifted. As Lindsay took it Piers said, 'You're honoured. Bruce won't do it for everybody.'

As they moved away, Lindsay turned to look at the house and exclaimed at the beautiful wistaria which covered a large part of the handsome building. Putting out a hand, she pulled a spray to her face and inhaled its wonderful scent. Smiling up at Piers, she caught a strange expression in his eyes.

Suddenly he said, 'Hold it,' and, drawing a small camera from his pocket, he took a quick snap. Smiling at her surprise, he said, 'A beautiful woman and a beautiful flower. Irresistible.'

There seemed nothing to say to this, but it was undeniably pleasant to receive such a compliment, and Lindsay glowed a little as they walked over the immaculate lawns. A few minutes later, returning to the house, he went to pour her a drink while she stood looking through a large window giving on to another part of the garden. Through blossoming trees she caught a glimpse of the River Thames and drew a long breath of appreciation. Taking the glass he handed her, she said, 'This Thames Valley area is so different from Devon where I grew up. It's more sophisticated, of course, but it has a charm of its own that's gradually growing on me.' She sipped her drink then looked up in surprise. 'Champagne! I always think of it as a celebration wine. Aren't you taking things rather for granted?'

He hesitated. 'Well—I really can't guess at your decision, but I'm enjoying your company so much that champagne is the only drink worthy of the occasion.'

'Goodness!' She smiled a little mockingly. 'You have a very smooth line in flattery.' Then as she met his eyes she turned hastily to the window. There was something in his expression that troubled her. This man was dangerously attractive, but she felt instinctively that she must resist his charm. He was, she strongly suspected, a man of many affairs and she had no wish to be one of his conquests.

Breaking into her thoughts, Piers said, 'Jim is bringing his wife with him. You've met her, haven't you?'

'Only once. The first evening I arrived she invited me for a drink, obviously to give me the once-over.' Remembering the searching questions to which she had been subjected, she added, 'I couldn't understand why she was so interested in me—after all, I was only coming for three months as a locum. You must have had other locums before. Do you think they were always put through such an examination?'

A nerve twitched in his cheek, but before answering he drew her gently towards a long mirror on the wall. Then he said, 'Look at yourself. Can't you see that you constitute a danger to any man?'

Turning quickly away, she stared at him.

'But—but Jim—Denise—they're nearing retirement age—that's absurd!'

He returned her incredulous gaze with a derisory smile.

'Not Jim. They have a son in the Army. Coming home soon on leave. A very susceptible young man. Gets into all kinds of entanglements. Denise is a possessive mother.'

Once more that word 'entanglement'—Lindsay burst out laughing.

'Well, forewarned is forearmed. I'll have no difficulty in putting this callow youth in his place if necessary. That's if he even looks twice at me.'

'Oh, Mark is no callow youth. He's an officer—a captain now, I think—based temporarily at Sandhurst.' Piers went over to a window looking down the drive.

'Here they are and—good lord, Mark must be home already! They've brought him along.'

He went out to meet them and Lindsay stood deep in thought. There had been something odd in Piers' voice—a hint of annoyance at the arrival of the man against whom he had been warning her? He seemed determined that she should keep her distance from his partner's son. Was the situation really as he had described? She smiled to herself. She would put it to the test and ignore his hints.

Much later, when she was back in her flat and getting ready for bed, she went over in her mind the events of the evening. Mark had turned out to be charming. He was tall, fair-haired, with laughing blue eyes, and he must, she had thought, be even more devastatingly handsome in uniform. She remembered, too, that Piers had shown obvious displeasure at the way in which she had apparently succumbed. What she had found strange was that his mother had shown no sign of possessiveness. In fact, she had seemed to be pleased that they were getting on so well.

The question of a permanency in the practice had been broached only briefly. Jim had taken her aside, asked her outright if she was interested, and she had told him she was grateful for the unexpected offer. That had seemed to satisfy him and the rest of the evening had been taken up with light-hearted conversation. In the middle of it all a telephone call had come for Piers, who had taken it outside the room and had come back looking irritated. Jim had laughingly asked if the call was from that glamorous rich widow who, rumour had it, was trying to hook him. Piers had shrugged it off but his eyes were angry. It was when

Mark had said jokingly that rich widows, especially glamorous ones, were not to be sneezed at that Lindsay had noticed Denise was the only one who did not join in the general laughter.

Following her puzzled glance, Mark said quietly, 'Ma doesn't like the idea of anyone angling for Piers. She has other plans for him.'

Astonished, she looked at him questioningly.

'What can your mother have to do with Piers? She's not related to him, is she?'

'Oh, no. But you see, it's rumoured that Piers will eventually have a handle to his name and Ma would like him for Fiona.'

'Fiona?' Lindsay was confused. 'Fiona who?'

Mark smiled sardonically. 'My young sister. Twenty years old. Working in Paris at the moment, but soon coming home for a holiday, much to Ma's joy.'

Lindsay laughed. 'Is your sister pretty?'

Mark shrugged. 'Not in your league.' He studied her in open admiration. 'I must say Piers is jolly lucky to have you working with him. I wonder if I could detach you from him? I've got ten days' leave. How about letting me take you out one evening? Several evenings, in fact.'

'I'm not attached to Piers in any way apart from work,' Lindsay said coolly, then, warming to Mark's charm, she added, 'I'd enjoy going out with you, but I'd have to arrange for time off.'

'Well, let's start with tomorrow evening.' He took her glass from her and placed it on a side-table, then turned towards Piers. 'Would you mind if Lindsay and I went for a stroll in your garden? It's such a lovely evening and the view from here looks enticing.'

There was a moment's hesitation, then Piers said calmly, 'A good idea. Let's all go.' He turned to his partner. 'Jim, I'd like your advice on that extra bit of land I've bought at the side of the house.'

'Cunning devil,' Mark said under his breath and Lindsay smiled to herself as they all drifted out on to the terrace. Gradually Mark drew her away from the others and led her down to where the garden looked over the river. It was beautiful and mysterious in the growing dusk. They stood for a while listening to the quiet lapping of the water against a small boat tied up to a landing-stage.

'I suppose that nifty little craft belongs to Piers.' Mark began to open the garden gate. 'How about it?'

'Oh, no!' Lindsay was alarmed. 'I'm sure Piers wouldn't like——'

'All right.' Mark laughed. 'Perhaps it wouldn't be quite the thing. So let's sit here——' He pointed to a wooden garden bench, drew her down beside him and placed his arm round her shoulders.

'You're so lovely,' he said softly, and drew her closer, but to her relief there was a sudden barking as Piers' dog bounded towards them, followed by the voices of the rest of the approaching party.

Now, as she got into bed, Lindsay remembered with amusement the sharpness in Piers' voice as he'd called the dog back and the irritated way in which Mark had said, 'Damn! He needn't have come this way. I suppose he suspects my motives towards you. But it's nothing to do with him. He should have more tact. Anyway, from what I hear he's no laggard in love himself. I guess it's a question of sour grapes.'

For a moment Lindsay's quiet smile faded as she

recalled that last phrase. For some reason it was vaguely depressing. Then, pushing the thought aside, she concentrated on Mark. It would be amusing to have a light-hearted flirtation with him. It would also be a pleasant diversion and brighten up her life, which, so far, had been ruled by serious concentration on her work. It was time to have a little fun.

In the morning she got up early and went into the surgery. To her surprise, Alison was already there. She laughed.

'It's Dracula. He's been on my mind all night, so here I am—unusually early. Look—true to his name, Dracula eats at night. He's pecked at his food and now he's gone to sleep again.'

'He's taken well over half the amount I put there,' Lindsay said. 'I shouldn't think there's much wrong with him or he wouldn't be interested.'

Alison nodded in agreement. 'You know, yesterday I said he gave me the creeps, but I must admit he's rather sweet. Pathetic, too, in the way he folds his wings about himself when he goes to sleep. Poor little thing. We must seem like giants to him—huge creatures from outer space. We look on this as our planet, but it's his as well.'

Suddenly the telephone rang and when Alison answered she turned to Lindsay and made a face. 'Yes—yes, Mrs Lockwood. I'm afraid he's not here yet—it's rather early for him to come in.' Putting her hand over the receiver, she whispered, 'She sounds in a fine temper. Demands to speak to Piers. Shall I tell her to ring his house?'

Lindsay shook her head and took the receiver. As soon as she announced herself, Mrs Lockwood snapped, 'It's Piers I want, but you might as well hear what I have to say as it concerns you. The Labrador you examined yesterday is not at all well. You said she was perfectly fit, but you were wrong. There is something very odd about her. She not her normal self.'

Lindsay kept her voice calm.

'I'll come over as soon as I've finished surgery, which will be——'

'No! I don't want you.' The interruption was bitingly cold. 'I don't think you know what you're doing. Piers must come as soon as possible. That's why I've rung so early. He must make it his first call.'

She rang off, leaving Lindsay staring angrily at the telephone. Turning to Alison, she was about to speak when the door opened and Piers said, 'You look upset. What's wrong?'

Lindsay drew a long breath.

'It's Mrs Lockwood. She wants you out first thing. Says the Labrador isn't well. She also told me that I'm not up to my job. She's very angry and so am I.'

Alison giggled and Lindsay turned on her. 'It's not a laughing matter. She'll probably tell all her wretched friends that I'm no good as a vet.'

Alison shrugged. 'Well, you needn't worry about that, need you? You're only doing a locum here, so she can't do you any real harm.'

Lindsay bit her lip, then, to her surprise, Piers said smoothly, 'I see no reason why you shouldn't know, Alison. Lindsay has agreed to stay on here permanently.'

'Oh! That's lovely!' Alison looked delighted but

Lindsay felt annoyed. She had purposely refrained from mentioning the subject to the nurses, thinking it best to wait until everything was settled. Then Alison said, 'Jessica's just come in—I'll go and give her the good news.'

There was silence for a few minutes then Piers asked, 'This business with Sophie's Labrador—what symptoms is the bitch showing?'

'I didn't get the chance to ask. In any case, she wouldn't discuss it with me. She just wants you there as soon as possible.' In spite of her anger at the memory, Lindsay couldn't help laughing. 'I'll bet she's making the whole thing up. It's you she wants—in more senses than one.' She paused and added mockingly, 'Oh, don't pretend you don't know what I mean—it's obvious to everyone. She's a spider intent on getting you into her web.'

'Good God!' Piers looked aghast. 'What a thing to say! You've certainly got your knife into her.'

She shrugged. 'It's the general opinion.'

'So I'm the subject of gossip. I must say——' He turned suddenly as the door opened. 'Jim—what's brought you here so early?'

The older man smiled. 'I wanted to catch you before you went on your rounds. Something has come up and I'm sure you'll be interested.' He turned to Lindsay. 'You too. A mare over at Mr Williams' stables is showing signs of EVA—Equine Viral Arteritis—the disease in which damage is caused to the arteries.' He paused. 'Better tell your nurses that it's nothing to do with arthritis. I think you should both come and see the mare as I'm pretty sure there will be more cases to come in the future.' He frowned. 'We, along with

Ireland and Japan, are the only countries in the world which have so far been free from EVA. It's a common problem in standard-bred trotting horses in Europe and North America.'

Piers nodded. 'I was reading about it only this week. Apparently a stallion was imported from Poland last year. It had been certified as free from EVA by the Polish authorities, but it's now believed to be the cause of the outbreak. It has recently been used for stud purposes in about twenty premises, so the mares which have been served by this stallion or have received his semen must be traced.' He paused. 'This particular mare—is she in foal?'

Jim nodded. 'Yes, and now she may well abort. Even if she doesn't, the infection will affect the foal. Do you know the symptoms?'

'I haven't seen a case yet, but from what I read in veterinary literature there is a raised temperature, conjunctivitis and a nasal discharge.'

Lindsay said quietly, 'Also oedema of the trunk and legs.'

Jim looked pleased. 'I see you've both kept yourselves up to date. Well, this mare had the first two symptoms yesterday and Mr Williams has just phoned to say it now has the nasal discharge.' He looked at his watch. 'I've arranged to be at the stables at eleven—time for you to do your most urgent calls and for you, Lindsay, to finish your morning surgery. Join me there.' He stopped on his way out. 'By the way, this stables is very near one of your clients, Piers— the one we teased you about last evening. Mrs Lockwood has two mares, hasn't she? You'll have to warn her as the disease can be passed from one mare to another without even coming into contact with the stallion.'

'Hmm, I suppose I'll have to tell her.' Piers shrugged resignedly. 'That means she'll be calling me out even more than she does now.'

His partner chuckled. 'She certainly likes your company. My wife says——' He stopped, then added apologetically, 'Well, there's not much that goes on in the practice that escapes my wife, you know.'

Lindsay turned aside to hide her amusement, but as Piers went out she caught sight of his face. Judging from his grim expression, Sophie Lockwood would be getting short shrift from him if there was absolutely nothing wrong with the Labrador.

Surgery was not very busy and luckily there were only two cats to spay afterwards. This operation Lindsay had down to a fine art. Once the anaesthetic had taken effect, she shaved a small amount of fur, made an incision of about an inch, drew out the ovaries and uterus, put an injection of antibiotic into the wound and stitched it up swiftly and expertly. As she washed her hands, she turned to the nurses. 'Twenty minutes to spare—just time for a quick coffee.'

Sitting over the hot drink, she discussed the suspect EVA case and Jessica said, 'I heard what Jim said about Mrs Lockwood. Piers will have his hands full with her neurotic imaginings.'

'She's not neurotic,' Alison said scornfully. 'It's all a ploy to get Piers. Mind you, there's one person who would hate him to fall for the glamorous widow. Denise has got her eye on him for her daughter.'

Jessica nodded. 'And Fiona is quite something. A red-haired beauty. Clever too. Actually, I should think she'd make a good wife for Piers. Of course, she may have other plans.' She glanced slyly at Lindsay and added, 'We've had a bet on her, but the odds have lengthened a bit since you came.'

Lindsay stiffened. 'Don't be so silly. No wonder Piers is so much against marriage if he finds everybody trying to hitch him up to every eligible female.' She got up. 'I must be off.' She turned as the door opened.

'I'm just in time, I see.' Mark stood smiling at her. 'I'd like to come with you to see that suspect horse. Pop was discussing it over the breakfast-table and said you and Piers would be going to see it. I'm at a loose end and I'm interested in horses, so will you let me come with you?'

Very conscious of the glances that were passing between Jessica and Alison, Lindsay found it difficult to hide her embarrassment. She hesitated. 'Well, I don't know whether you'll be very welcome at the stables. They might not like——'

'Oh, they won't object. Friends of mine. Their son went to school with me.'

Lindsay shrugged resignedly. 'OK. It's up to you. I'll see you there, then.'

'I must hitch a lift from you. My car's being serviced.' He grinned amiably. 'I'll drive if you like. Get you there in no time.'

'No, thanks,' Lindsay said firmly. 'I'd like to get there in one piece.' She paused. 'I hope your father and Piers won't think it's my idea that you should come.'

Reluctantly, she allowed him to follow her out to her car and, as he settled himself beside her, he said, 'Come on. Unbend a bit. I thought we were going to be friends.'

Despite her irritation, she gradually relaxed and by the time they arrived at the stables the atmosphere between them was warm and friendly. Parking her car next to the others, she got out and looked around, wondering which way to go.

Mark pointed. 'Over there—the stable block. I expect that's where they are.'

She gave him a quick glance as they walked down the gravel path. 'Why are you so interested in this new disease? Do you keep a horse yourself?'

'No. But as a vet's son I've always had a hankering for the profession and sometimes regret that I didn't become a vet myself.' He paused. 'However, I'm very happy in the Army. The only trouble is that it's not all that easy to find a girl who likes that kind of life. It's not a very settled existence.'

Lindsay laughed mockingly. 'I find that hard to believe. How many girls have you actually asked?'

He hesitated, then grinned. 'I've never yet met one I've wanted to marry.' As they turned a corner into the stable block, he added very softly, 'Up till now, that is.'

Whether she was meant to hear that or not, she realised suddenly that she must tread carefully if she didn't want to get too involved. He was, her instinct told her, an accomplished flirt and shouldn't be taken too seriously. He probably moved easily from one affair to another—rather like Piers, except that Mark maintained he was looking for a wife, whereas Piers was openly against marriage. Then her reflections came to an end at the sight of Jim and Piers and as the former came to meet them he raised his eyebrows at the sight of his son.

Turning to Piers, he murmured something, gave a

short laugh then said, 'Didn't expect you. Why this sudden interest in veterinary matters?'

Mark shrugged. 'Well, being on leave, it's nice to see other people working.'

'Hmm.' His father's gaze travelled to Lindsay and he said, 'All the same, you'd better not come to see the mare. Jack Summers is hopping mad and doesn't want the bad news spread abroad.'

'OK,' Mark said easily. 'I'll hang around till you've finished. See you later.'

He turned away, and his father added, 'We're all going in for a drink in the house so we'll meet there.'

A few minutes later, Lindsay stood looking at the sick mare, and listened carefully while Jim pointed out the signs of EVA.

'See how the legs and trunk are swelling? That, combined with the other symptoms, confirms the diagnosis.' He turned to the groom, a short, stocky man who was shaking his head gloomily at the bad news. 'You'll have to keep her isolated for about three weeks, though even then——' he frowned '—even then there's no guarantee that the others won't catch it, as it can also be spread by the respiratory route. Of course, all equipment such as grooming brushes and rugs must be kept separate.' He turned. 'Ah, here's Mr Summers himself.'

A tall, burly man with a florid complexion under a mane of grey hair came towards them and raised bushy eyebrows at their serious faces.

'You don't need to tell me. Is it notifiable?'

'No.' Jim shook his head. 'The responsibility for dealing with it lies with the owner. One ray of hope.

Research is going on to produce an inactivated vaccine against the virus. And in America a live virus vaccine has been licensed against EVA, but not yet in the European Community.'

'Let's hope we can control it without recourse to vaccination,' Mr Summers said, and added fiercely, 'I'd like to get hold of the exporter of that stallion from Poland. The standards of testing there are obviously not reliable. It also raises doubts about protection against other animal diseases.' He subsided, but not before muttering angrily about the EC and open frontiers, with Jim nodding in thoughtful agreement.

'What will happen to the culprit?' Lindsay asked, and Mr Summers shrugged.

'He'll be castrated, of course. The stallion, I mean— not the exporter.'

The resultant laughter lightened the atmosphere and Mr Summers said, 'Let's go in and drink to that.'

As they moved towards the house, Mark came round the corner and Mr Summers greeted him jovially, 'Home on leave, eh? Come and join us. Pity Simon isn't here. Strange to think he's married now. You going in for matrimony yet?'

Mark shot a quick glance at Lindsay and shrugged the question away, but she turned to look behind her as though she hadn't heard Mark, only to meet Piers' gaze. To her surprise, he was frowning so deeply that she could only conclude that he was concentrating on the EVA case. She waited until he caught up with her then asked, 'Are you worried that Mrs Lockwood's mares could get the EVA infection?'

His frown disappeared, but his voice was cold. 'Well,

she'll have to be warned and be very watchful. By the
way—that Labrador. Nothing wrong at all, but Sophie
insists that there is. So I gave an injection just to stop
her pestering.' He smiled drily. 'It was only a placebo,
so I shan't charge her for it.' He flushed suddenly as
he saw a momentary flash of scorn in Lindsay's eyes.
'What else could I do?' he demanded sharply.

'Well, you could tell her to get another vet,' she
mocked him gently. 'You shake your head—obviously
you rather like——' She stopped as she saw an angry
glint in his eyes and moved away quickly to catch up
with the others.

Once they were inside the house the talk was mainly
about horses, so much so that Mark eventually came
up to Lindsay looking rather bored. He said, 'This is
all very well but I have something more important on
my mind.' He paused and looked at her hopefully. 'I
want to take you out somewhere. When's your
day off?'

She smiled at his eagerness. 'It depends. I'm only a
locum so it varies.'

'All the same, will you keep the next one for me?'

She pondered. 'Well, not the whole day. And, of
course, if an emergency arose, I'd have to be available.'

'Taking that into account, what about the evenings?
Dinner somewhere—say, tonight? Oh, come on,
Lindsay—my leave is getting shorter. Take pity on
me.'

'Goodness! How dramatic!' she teased him gently,
but he didn't respond in the same vein.

'Lindsay, I'm serious. I want——' He broke off as
Piers suddenly appeared.

'Lindsay, I have to see a cow with suspected aceto-

naemia. It's on the way back to the surgery. Would
you like to see it?'

Eager to enlarge her experience, she exclaimed, 'Oh,
yes! It will be interesting.' Then she paused and turned
to Mark. 'Would you mind waiting in my car outside
the farm?'

Before he could answer, Piers said, 'No need for
that. Lindsay can come in my car and you can drive
hers back. Is that OK, Lindsay?'

Rather reluctantly she nodded, and Mark shrugged
resignedly. Then, turning his back on Piers, he said
pointedly, 'I'll come for you at seven-thirty this
evening,' and walked away so quickly that she had no
time to tell him that she would be on call.

'Hmm.' Piers raised his eyebrows. 'Before you ask,
yes, I'll stand in for you this evening.'

She flushed. 'I hadn't actually planned——'

'Sweeping you off your feet, is he? Somehow I don't
see you as an army wife.'

She burst out laughing. 'Really, Piers—you seem to
have a fixation about marriage. An invitation to
dinner—nothing serious in that.'

He relaxed. 'You're right, of course. I must get used
to my beautiful assistant being surrounded by admiring
males. Come to think of it, I might as well join the
queue. Will you consider a date with me?' Seeing her
hesitation, he added mockingly, 'You needn't look so
doubtful. I'm not dangerous.'

'I wasn't thinking like that. I was wondering how
we could both be absent from the practice at the
same time.'

'If that's your only objection, we can easily overcome
it by going somewhere local. Don't forget my mobile

phone.' He paused. 'Here in the Thames Valley there are lots of pleasant places—riverside restaurants, local theatres where shows are given a pre-London run— you have only to name your preference.'

She laughed. 'You make it sound very alluring. I must say I do like this part of the world.'

He looked pleased. 'Another alternative. How would you like to come out on the river? I know all the quiet backwaters. Very romantic.'

'I'm not looking for romance,' she cut him down swiftly, then relented. 'Well, I do love the water, so perhaps——' She broke off, then, without thinking, she added smilingly, 'The evening we all met in your house and Mark and I walked down to the river we saw your boat. It looked so inviting that Mark suggested we should steal a ride.'

Piers' mouth set in a grim line. 'What a nerve! I'd have had something to say about that. These army types—they think they can do what the hell they like.'

Hurriedly Lindsay came to Mark's defence. 'Oh, he was only joking. I wish I hadn't told you—now you'll dislike him even more.'

His eyebrows rose. 'What makes you think I dislike him?'

She shrugged. 'Well, you sound as though you do when you say "these army types".' She paused then added mischievously, 'Personally I find him rather attractive.'

His eyes narrowed. 'That's probably why I don't care for him much. Just an instinctive antagonism to him as a man.' He paused. 'I suppose it's jealousy.'

Lindsay stared and was about to retort sharply when

he exclaimed, 'Good lord! Here I am chatting away as though time didn't exist when I should be at Woodend Farm. Let's go.'

CHAPTER THREE

ONCE in Piers' car Lindsay reflected with amusement how quickly the atmosphere between them could change. One moment it was on a personal level—too personal at times—and the next, when the needs of an animal took over, the mutual interest they shared drove away all tension. Though why there should be any tension at all was puzzling. She was not usually uneasy with men. She liked their company when they were interesting and well-informed. As for falling in love, that, so far, hadn't happened. She smiled to herself. Love could wait—her freedom was very precious to her.

Suddenly she realised that Piers had asked her a question and her smile faded. 'Sorry,' she said. 'I was far away.'

His tone was dry. 'Judging from your smile, I imagine your thoughts were far removed from me. I asked you if you liked large-animal work as much as treating small animals?'

'That's a difficult question. I like variety. I've been doing locum work for some while now, but I've never had much practical experience with large animals. It's understandable, I suppose, but it seems a pity that women don't often get the chance to prove their worth with farmers.'

'A bit of a feminist, are you?' He sounded amused.

She retorted sharply, 'You needn't be so patronising.

Of course I'm a feminist. Most women are. It's only through fighting our way through male prejudice that we've got where we are today.'

'OK, I'm not prejudiced. If I were I wouldn't be showing you the large-animal side of our practice.' He turned the car into a lane which led up to a closed farm gate. Getting out, he opened it, drove through then stopped again. This time, in spite of his protest, Lindsay got out first and closed it behind them.

Back in the car, she asked, 'Any more gates?'

'One more—round the bend. I'll open it, you shut it. Good idea, this equality.' Before moving off he turned to her, laughter in his eyes, and suddenly his arm was round her and his lips were pressing on hers in a long, hard kiss.

She was gasping as she drew back and stared at him. 'What on earth brought that on?'

He looked troubled as he gripped the steering-wheel. He said slowly, 'I really don't know. I suppose it was because—because——' He stopped, then said drily, 'You must work it out for yourself.'

She waited for an apology, but he said no more until they came to the next gate, when he observed calmly, 'Good, it's open,' and a few moments later they were in the farmyard.

The farmer looked worried as he led them towards a loose box. 'I'm half afraid it might be BSE.'

'Tell me the symptoms again,' Piers said. 'What was the first thing you noticed?'

'Well, the milk secretion was reduced, then she ceased to feed normally and seemed very depressed, though every now and then there were odd periods when she became excited. That's when I began to wonder about BSE. I've never had a case so far.' He grinned ruefully. 'My wife says I've got it on the brain—"mad cow disease", as they call it—but it seems to me that those symptoms are ominous.'

Piers shook his head. 'There's a test—Rothera's test—that can be carried out, but I don't think that's necessary. I can diagnose it from here. That smell—it's unmistakable.' He went up to the cow and put his face close to the animal's mouth. Then he drew back and gestured to the farmer. 'Take a long breath—do you get it? A sickly sweet odour—acetone. It's all over her and it'll be in the urine, in the milk and even in the skin.' He paused. 'How many calves has she had?'

The farmer thought for a moment. 'Three so far.'

Piers nodded. 'That's about right. It seldom occurs before the third calving. It's a metabolic disturbance that occurs whenever the glucose level in the blood plasma is low.' He paused. 'Now, you've been feeding her silage, haven't you? Is it good quality?'

The other man frowned. 'Well, it wasn't the best. Surely that's not the reason?'

'It's a pre-disposing factor. Along with my treatment, I'd like you to give her cut grass with the addition of a little molasses, and she must have exercise—that will aid recovery. Now——' he bent down to open his case '—I'll give her a glucose solution injection——' he filled a syringe '—and come back tomorrow to give another. If that doesn't work, then I'll have to use cortico-steroids, though I hope it won't be necessary.' He smiled at the expression of relief on the farmer's face and added, 'If your sense of smell isn't very good, get your wife to take a sniff. She'll recognise it if she varnishes her nails—you know—acetone.'

The farmer grinned. 'Well, as you know, I haven't been at this farming lark very long. I used to be a beekeeper—had a pretty good commercial honey farm, but my father died and left me this farm, so now I've cut down the number of my hives and just enjoy it as a hobby.'

Piers said, 'I find that very interesting. I've got three hives of my own. If I have a problem I'll know where to come to find a solution.'

Back in the car, Lindsay said, 'Thank you for letting me go with you—it was very instructive.' She paused. 'Interesting, too, about the bees. Where do you keep them?'

'On a piece of land at the side of my garden. I've kept them for years. Fascinating. Do you know anything about them?'

'No. But I'd like to. They're wonderfully intelligent, aren't they?'

He shook his head vehemently. 'No intelligence at all. They're guided solely by instinct. The individual bee has no mind as we understand the term. All the activities of the hive are wholly instinctive and performed without the slighest gleam of conscious intelligence. They do their work according to laws as fixed as those which govern the courses of the stars.' He paused. 'If you are really interested I'd love to show them to you and explain the amazing way in which a colony is organised. I'll fix a day—a fine day—and we'll watch the bees all working away for me, though they don't know it.'

She laughed and said impulsively, 'You're full of surprises. Somehow I never imagined you as having such a hobby.'

He shot her a quick sideways glance. 'How did you imagine me?'

That was a question to which she could find no possible response and she shrugged lightly, as though it was of no importance. For a moment the atmosphere between them seemed charged with electricity and Lindsay could feel her heart beating unevenly. Confused, she said at last, 'Actually I've not thought much about you at all. It's only recently that I've come to know you.'

'And do you like what you know?'

This was even more difficult to answer but she said calmly, 'That's a bit too personal.'

He nodded slowly. 'Perhaps. For my part, I find that the more I know you, the more I'm intrigued. I have the feeling that——' He stopped abruptly and she saw his hand tighten on the steering-wheel. 'Well, you're a kind of challenge.' He paused. 'That's not quite what I mean. I can't find the right word. Perhaps "temptation" would be better.'

Lindsay stiffened. Then, as the memory of his sudden kiss of an hour ago came vividly into her mind, she felt a surge of anger. She said sharply, 'Don't talk such nonsense. You're making me out to be a kind of *femme fatale*, which I certainly am not.' She paused then added scornfully, 'I suppose that's your usual line of talk to any presentable girl. Well, it doesn't work with me.'

'Ouch!' He grinned ruefully. 'You certainly know how to slap a man down. Let me tell you I've never said that to a woman before. What's more, I'll never say it to you again.'

'Thank goodness for that,' Lindsay said coldly.

'Now we know where we stand.'

The silence lasted until they reached the surgery then as he pulled up he said, 'I'm coming in to have a look at the bat,' and Lindsay reflected that professional interest had, once more, taken over.

As they entered the surgery the nurses greeted them cheerfully.

Alison said, 'Dracula is doing well. He's taken food and water and now, as you can see, he's climbed to the top of the cage, folded his wings and gone to sleep.'

'Let's see how the wound is healing.' Piers put on gloves and reached into the cage. Supporting the bat with one hand, he examined the wing and then each limb in turn. 'Good. We can probably release him in a few days' time.' He paused as he studied the little creature. 'See how his arms and legs are enclosed in living webbing which flies superbly. If you took away the webbing, you would see a little animal with two arms and hands and two hind legs. They have the same number of fingers as we have, but they're formed differently. The thumb is very short, and instead of a nail it has this claw or hook which enables it to walk or hang on to anything where it can fold its wings and go to sleep.'

As he replaced his patient, Lindsay asked, 'How will you release it? Take it into the open and let it go?'

'Oh, no. We must wait till dark then take it back to the churchyard where it can join its mates.'

He turned to leave then stopped and looked steadily at Lindsay. 'I hope you enjoy your evening with Mark.' He smiled at the nurses. 'I'll be on call, so contact me if anything comes up.'

He shut the door behind him, leaving Jessica and Alison looking openly curious. Jessica murmured, 'Nice work,' and Alison said,

'Tell us, please. Brighten up our lives.'

Lindsay burst out laughing. 'It's no big deal. I was rather conned into it but I suppose I'll have to go now that Piers has said he'll stand in for me.'

'Where's Mark taking you?'

'I haven't the faintest idea.' Lindsay shrugged. 'He said something about dinner. That's all I know.'

And that was what puzzled her when, after evening surgery, she went up to her flat to get ready. What on earth to wear? At last she decided to play safe and wear her new pale green dress. She had gasped at the price when she'd bought it, but on the strength of the very good salary she was getting here she had rather guiltily treated herself.

Mark was prompt, arriving in his mother's car, for which he apologised as Lindsay got into the passenger seat.

'This model is a bit staid, but my car won't be ready till tomorrow. I've booked a table at the Swallow's Nest, a riverside hotel which is well-known for its cuisine.' He paused. 'Unfortunately there's no dancing there until the weekend, but next time when you have your day off we'll do a theatre in London then go on to a nightclub for dancing. Would you like that?' He glanced at her before turning the ignition key. 'Oh, don't look so doubtful. Surely you'd like to take advantage of the fact that we're within reach of London's bright lights?' His eyes swept over her approvingly. 'With you dressed like that I'd be proud to show you off. In fact——' He stopped, then said slowly, 'Will you come to the officers' mess one evening? I'd like you to meet my CO!'

Lindsay stiffened. She said coldly, 'Meet your CO? Why on earth would you want me to do that?'

'Well. . .' He started the engine, then, with his eyes fixed on the road ahead, he said quietly, 'They like to vet their officers' future——'

He got no further. Lindsay gasped and sat bolt upright.

'Mark, you can't possibly think—you must be joking.'

'No,' he said firmly. 'No joke. I knew from the moment I saw you that I wanted to marry you.'

She made a great effort to keep her voice steady. 'You're being far too impulsive. You don't know me, or I you, for that matter. I'm going to forget what you've just said.'

'OK, we'll leave it for a bit,' he said calmly. 'All the same, before my leave is up I'll ask you again. Will you give it serious thought, please? Promise?'

She hesitated. 'I don't know—oh, all right. But don't let's talk about it this evening, otherwise I shall regret having come out with you.'

'I can't promise that. I want to put all the pros and cons to you. About being an army wife, I mean.'

'I shan't enjoy the evening, then,' she said sharply. 'In fact I'd rather go back.'

'Too late.' He grinned at her. 'See—we're here. Look—isn't this just perfect?'

He turned the car into a parking space and, in spite of her irritation, Lindsay's mood softened. It was a beautiful place—a long, low building, its walls covered with honeysuckle and budding roses. Down the side she caught a glimpse of smooth green lawns sweeping down to a wide stretch of the Thames.

Seated at a table by a picture window, Lindsay decided to get the conversation moving on lines of her own choice. Accordingly, as soon as they had made their choice from the menu and Mark had ordered the wine, she said, 'You said your sister is coming back from Paris. Your parents will be glad to have her home, I expect. Tell me about her.'

He shrugged and grinned. 'Fiona is—well, Fiona. Just coming up for her twenty-first birthday. Quite pretty—rather striking, in fact. Reddish hair, eyes that flash at you if she doesn't get her own way. Which she usually does.'

Lindsay laughed. 'A typical brotherly description. Does she have lots of men friends?'

'They're like bees round the proverbial honey pot but, as far as we know, she's not serious about any of them. Mind you, nobody knows what she gets up to in Paris. Ma has plans for her, but I don't think she'll succeed in getting Fiona to fall in line. She never has, so far.' He stopped. 'Now let's talk about someone more interesting. You for instance.'

'But I find your sister interesting,' Lindsay said firmly. 'What plans has your mother got in mind?'

'Oh, Ma wants to make a match between Piers and Fiona,' he said airily. 'Personally, I don't think she's got a hope.'

Remembering the gossip in the surgery, Lindsay decided to have it confirmed. She asked, 'Is that because your mother wants to keep an interest in the practice when your father retires?'

'Good lord, no.' Mark paused. 'It's rumoured that one day Piers will have a handle to his name. I'm not so sure, but Ma is very ambitious socially.'

Lindsay nodded, trying to keep the conversation going, but her heart sank when Mark said resolutely, 'Now, let's get back to us. You may think I'm rushing things but I'm a fast worker. Do you think you could come to care for me? I'm not asking for much—just a little hope.'

She studied him carefully. Nice-looking, very direct in his speech and perhaps a little over-confident of his ability to sweep a girl off her feet. A pleasant, amusing friend, but as a lover and husband—definitely not. She shook her head.

'I can't give you any hope, Mark. I like you very much, but I don't love you and I know I never will.'

'How do you know—how can you be so sure? You're obviously the cautious type—I realise I'll have to take things more slowly.' He paused. 'Sandhurst isn't far away, so I'll come over at every opportunity, and for the rest of my leave I'll see you whenever you're free.'

Lindsay began to feel apprehensive. It was flattering that he should be so determined, but she knew she would never want more than a pleasant friendship. She was going to have her work cut out to discourage him.

After dinner they strolled along the riverbank, and Mark, sensing her reluctance, had the tact not to take advantage of the romantic surroundings. They exchanged a cool kiss in the moonlight and then he drove her back.

'I'll come round tomorrow after evening surgery,' he said firmly. 'We'll go out for a drink somewhere.'

And, ignoring her protest that she would not be free, he smiled and drove away.

The thought of his persistence worried her all the following day, in spite of the fact that she was kept very busy. She was seeing her last patient of evening surgery when Piers walked in, nodded smilingly and went into the office. To her surprise, she realised that her heart was racing. It was as though his presence affected her in a disturbing way. Hurriedly dismissing the thought and stroking the young cat on the table, she turned to his anxious owners.

'Just because Tom's mother died from feline leukaemia it doesn't mean that he has inherited it. The tests show no symptoms and there are no outward signs—loss of condition, poor appetite, anaemia et cetera. However, just to be on the safe side, now that a vaccine is available, I think it would be a good idea to immunise him against the disease. Would you like me to give him this injection?'

As soon as they consented, Lindsay filled a syringe and a few minutes later, with promises to bring Tom back in three months' time for examination, the clients departed.

As the door closed behind them, Piers came out of the office.

'I've had Sophie Lockwood on the phone. She's in a complete panic about the EVA in her neighbour's stables. I've told her there is no preventative vaccine available yet, but she wants me to look in every day to make sure her mares are still in the clear. I said that if I was very busy you would go in my place. She nearly went through the roof at first, but when I suggested she should try another vet she climbed

down.' He paused. 'Will you help me out from time
to time?'

Lindsay hesitated then said reluctantly, 'I haven't
any option, have I? It's not that I mind examining
the horses—that's interesting—but if Mrs Lockwood is
rude to me I shall be hard put to it not to let fly at her.'

Piers looked amused. 'That might be just what
she needs.' He frowned. 'I can't think why she
dislikes you.'

Alison, hovering near by, tried unsuccessfully to
stifle a giggle and he looked at her curiously. 'Do you
know why?'

She shrugged. 'It's obvious. She's jealous.'

'Jealous? How do you mean? Because Lindsay
is a vet?'

'No, of course not. She's—well——' Alison caught
a warning frown from Jessica '—she probably
thinks——' Once more she stopped, then finished
lamely, 'Lindsay is much more attractive—prettier—
than Mrs Lockwood.'

Piers stared at her blankly for a moment, then
shrugged.

'Women!' he said scornfully, then as the nurses
expostulated loudly he held out his hands in mock-
surrender. 'OK, OK! I apologise for the sexist remark.'
He turned to Lindsay. 'Will you come into the office,
please? I won't keep you long.'

As he shut the door behind her, she saw his mouth
twist at the corner, then he smiled.

'If you remember, I said I'd like to join the queue
of your—well, to use an old-fashioned word, admirers.
So will you come out with me tomorrow evening?
Dinner somewhere.'

She blinked in surprise. 'That's nice of you.' She paused, thinking fast as she remembered that Mark had said he would be coming to see her whenever he could. She smiled. 'Thank you. Though really you don't have to take me out to dinner. It's such lovely weather—how about a stroll by the river? I'd like that.'

'Just the thing.' He looked pleased. 'But not a stroll. My boat—how about that? I'll get my housekeeper to make up a picnic. Leave everything to me.'

It sounded delightful and Lindsay carried the pleasant prospect in her mind as she went up to her flat.

Preparing an omelette and salad, she was startled by a ring at her doorbell. Irritated, she remembered Mark and his resolve to take her out that evening and, frowning, she went to open up.

He stood there with a huge bunch of mixed flowers and smiled a little too confidently for her liking. Reluctantly she stood back to let him in. Taking the flowers, she thanked him coolly, then said, 'I'm sorry I can't invite you to share my meal. I haven't any more eggs.'

He laughed. 'You know full well why I've come. We'll go to that new restaurant round the corner. I hear it's rather good.'

'No, Mark. Thank you, but I have things to do here this evening. I can't possibly go out with you. You mustn't monopolise me like this.'

His face fell. 'Well, tomorrow evening, then.'

'No.' She paused. 'Actually I have another date. I'm going out with Piers.'

'What? Oh, that's a bit much. Lindsay, you can't! You're destined for me.'

She burst out laughing. 'Don't talk such nonsense,

Mark. I made my position clear last evening. I'm free and want to stay that way.'

He glowered at her. Then suddenly he relaxed and grinned ruefully. 'Well, let's hope you say the same thing to Piers. Though from what I hear he won't be offering marriage. He believes in loving 'em and leaving 'em. He wants to have his cake and eat it.' He paused. 'All right, I'll go, so no need to glare at me like that.' He went to the door, then turned. 'By the way, my sister arrived this afternoon. She brought a friend with her—a French girl. You'll meet them soon. Ma is going to throw a welcoming party on Saturday. I'll fetch you about eight.'

'Mark! I couldn't possibly. It's obviously a family affair—your mother hasn't invited me.'

'She leaves it to us to invite whom we like. I'm inviting you.'

He closed the door, leaving Lindsay staring after him. Exasperated at his possessive manner, she realised it was going to be difficult to shake him off. Turning back to her cooking, she made the omelette and sat down to her meal, resolving to solve the problem. It was to be hoped that he would eventually get tired of having his invitations refused. Subconsciously she knew he would not be inconsolable for long.

Her thoughts turned to Piers. Mark's rather snide remarks caused a slight chill, but she dismissed that with the thought that she was quite capable of looking after herself. The weather seemed settled—a picnic on the river would be lovely.

Full of anticipation, she busied herself with a few preparations. First of all, the right clothes—cream cotton shorts with a navy blue shirt and a soft woollen sweater in case it grew cold. Piers probably would wear much the same thing. He would be doing the rowing as the boat was a light skiff, and the prospect of sitting in the stern watching him pulling on the oars gave her a feeling she found impossible to define. She sat dreaming for a few minutes, then, taking a firm grip on herself, she dismissed him from her mind.

CHAPTER FOUR

NEXT morning there were lots of clients in the waiting-room and their pets were varied and rather noisy. One ragged-looking little mongrel gave vent at regular intervals to high-pitched yelps, causing three other dogs to growl restlessly and lunge towards him, while his owner, a lanky, untidy youth, sat unconcernedly reading a magazine. In the interests of peace and quiet, and with the other clients' permission, Alison led the noisy patient in first. Once on the examination table he submitted silently to Lindsay's gentle hands. She turned to his owner.

'Was it just a booster injection you needed for him?'

He nodded. 'That's what the bloke told me—the one who sold him to me. He says dogs have got to have their injection once a year.'

Lindsay nodded. 'Have you ever kept a dog before?'

'No.' He shrugged. 'My dad doesn't like animals, but now that I've left home I fancied having a dog. I'm out of work so I've got plenty of time to exercise him.' He dug into a pocket. 'I've got his vaccination card here. He's four years old. I think he's got fleas—he's always scratching. Can you do anything about that?'

Lindsay inserted a needle quickly into the scruff of the dog's neck and massaged it briskly, then she said, 'I'll de-flea him myself, then if you watch me you can have the rest of the stuff and do him yourself next time. Read the instructions carefully and don't overdo it. Mind you protect his eyes.'

That done, she added, 'He's not in very good condition. He needs worming. I'll give you some worming tablets.'

The youth looked alarmed. 'How much are they? I can't afford a lot of fancy things.'

'This won't break you.' Lindsay smiled. 'You can have the worming tablets for nothing. They're not just to keep your dog healthy, they're also to prevent the spread of Toxocara—that's a parasite that can cause blindness in children. They play in public places— parks et cetera, and dogs with roundworms sometimes carry this disease in their faeces. It's comparatively rare, but it's a risk that shouldn't be taken.'

The youth looked scornful. 'People shouldn't let their kids play with dogs' mess.'

'Obviously, but it could be accidental.' She handed over the necessary packet, charged him less than usual for the injection and the youth went away looking pleased.

The next client looked anxious. 'We're going abroad for a month so Sammy has to go into kennels. But last time we did that he came back with kennel cough. It's such a dreadful sound—people stop and look accusing. I've heard that there's some sort of preventative which stops dogs from getting it. Do you know what it is?'

Lindsay nodded. 'Yes. It's called Intrac. Given intranasally—in the nostrils. Would you like me to do it now?'

The client agreed and the nurses came forward to help. In their firm hold the corgi received a squirt in each nostril, much to his indignation and his owner's satisfaction.

Surgery continued with the usual succession of skin problems, bronchial troubles and booster injections, until Lindsay found herself hoping for a case that required surgery. But it was not to be and at last, with a sigh of relief, she sat down to a reviving coffee. Picking up the mug, she said thoughtfully, 'I wonder sometimes if people realise how much we should be thankful for the discovery of antibiotics. In the old days so many lives—human and animal—were lost by post-operative infections and all kinds of diseases. I think antibiotics are the greatest step forward in modern medicine.'

'Quite a speech.' Piers came forward from the doorway. 'We'll have to get you to give a talk to our local organisations.' He smiled as he poured out a coffee and added, 'By the way, I hear Fiona—Jim's daughter—has arrived and brought a friend with her. A French girl. According to Mark, she's an absolute stunner. I mention this because he said the girls would be coming in here soon. Fiona wants to show Giselle round.' He paused, and gazed at the nurses meaningly. 'Now, I shall be out on my calls. Very, very busy.' He grinned. 'You get the message? The list is beside the telephone. That's for your benefit, but I don't want to be chased by Fiona and her friend.' He gulped down his coffee and made for the door, where he paused. 'Don't forget this evening, Lindsay.'

When he'd gone Alison glanced at Jessica and Lindsay said calmly, 'Piers is going to take me for a picnic on the river. It should be nice.'

Alison opened her eyes wide. 'A romantic evening.

Lucky you. I wonder——?' She glanced again at
Jessica, then, just as Lindsay was going to deny the
prospect of romance, the telephone rang and Jessica
picked it up.

She listened, then shook her head. 'No, he's just
left to go on his calls. Would you like to speak to
Lindsay?'

She handed the receiver over and whispered, 'It's
Denise; she sounds cross.'

There was indeed irritation in the partner's
wife's voice.

'I'm sorry I've missed Piers. My daughter and her
friend were hoping he would be able to take them with
him on his calls. Jim isn't available. Well, it can't be
helped. You'll be able to show Giselle round the
surgery, won't you?'

Lindsay smiled to herself. 'Yes, I'll be here and I'm
looking forward to meeting your daughter. From what
I hear she's a lovely girl and very interesting.'

'Interesting? Well, yes, but difficult at times.' Denise
paused. 'I've just had a thought. Perhaps you could
give her the address of the farms where Piers will
be—the girls might like to drive out and see him
at work.'

Replacing the telephone, Lindsay looked thoughtful.
Denise was very transparent in her anxiety to get Piers
and Fiona together, and it seemed that Piers was
equally anxious to avoid being caught. It was really
rather amusing. Just as she was turning away, the telephone sounded again and she found herself talking to
Mrs Lockwood.

'Piers hasn't arrived yet. I do think he might come
on time.'

'He's on his way, Mrs Lockwood. Should be with you in about ten minutes.'

'Well, thank goodness for that.' Mrs Lockwood rang off and Lindsay shrugged to herself, then sighed as once more the telephone rang.

This time it was Piers himself, talking on his mobile phone. 'Lindsay, I'm nearly at Sophie's place and I've been thinking. Will you or the nurses ring her in half an hour and say there's an emergency waiting anxiously for me?'

She laughed derisively. 'Can't you get away from her without all that performance?'

'Just do as I ask, please,' he said sharply, and rang off.

Jessica and Alison dissolved into laughter at the thought of Piers' dislike of being chased by Fiona and his need to be rescued from Mrs Lockwood.

Jessica said, 'Actually it's the first time he's been free. He broke off a long affair several months ago. At least, that's what we heard.'

'Not exactly a man to be trusted,' Lindsay said acidly, then added briskly, 'You needn't grin at each other like that. I know I'm going out with him this evening but I'm not pursuing him and he knows it.'

'Ah,' Alison said knowingly, 'but is he pursuing you?'

'Absolutely not,' Lindsay said emphatically, then added, 'At least not in the way you mean. We're both vets and we have that in common, so it's only a professional friendship.'

She turned away, but not before she heard Alison murmur, 'Professional friendship—I wonder? What are they going on the river for—to study the fish?'

Lindsay smiled wryly to herself. Of course, Alison was right. Piers, on his own admission, had joined what he called 'the queue' of her 'admirers'. So why had she accepted his invitation? Well, why not? She didn't want to be a workaholic and she liked men friends, just as long as they didn't become too ardent.

Twenty minutes later a car drew up in the yard and Jessica, standing by the window, said, 'Here they are—Fiona and her friend. Come and see.'

Giving way to curiosity, Lindsay glanced out and saw a tall, slim, red-haired girl and her small, raven-haired companion get out of what she recognised as Denise's car.

Alison said admiringly, 'They set each other off, don't they? I can just imagine them in Paris. What a time they must have.'

Jessica agreed. 'I can't see Fiona settling down here, much as her mother would like her to.' She turned away. 'Come on, we'd better look busy.'

Lindsay said calmly, 'No need to put on an act. They haven't come to spy. In any case, we've nothing to hide.'

'No.' Alison laughed. 'They've come to chase Piers. Denise won't like it if Piers falls for the French girl, though.'

Lindsay was thinking much the same thing as she watched the two girls walk across the yard. Giselle had that indefinable chic that seemed to be typical of French women. She was dressed like Fiona, in jeans and a T-shirt, but whereas Fiona's top was white Giselle's was black and clinging. A scarlet silk scarf was tied loosely round her neck, which emphasised the ivory pallor of her face. She was talking vivaciously as they came into the surgery and then stopped at the sight of the three girls awaiting them.

Fiona spoke first, greeting the nurses by name and acknowledging Lindsay with a smile. Then she said rather mischievously, 'I know what you're going to do: you're going to give me the addresses of the calls Piers is making this morning, aren't you?'

Lindsay nodded and reached out for the pad by the telephone.

'No—it's not necessary. We don't want to know. We've got other plans.' Fiona turned to her friend. 'That's so, isn't it, Giselle?'

The other girl nodded, her dark eyes gleaming with amusement. 'One does not always want to do what the good parents arrange. We have ideas of our own.'

Fiona laughed at Lindsay's puzzled look. 'It's OK. We're not awfully keen on the thought of following Piers around the farms. We're going shopping, then we're meeting Mark for lunch.'

Giselle's face lit up. 'Ah, yes! Your charming brother. I find him——' She searched for the right word and Fiona supplied it for her in friendly mockery.

'Dishy,' she said.

'"Dishy"—that is a word I find incomprehensible, but if it means that I find him very much to my taste then you are correct. I feel about him as you do about my cousin Pierre.'

'Shh!' Fiona said sharply. 'Giselle, you promised not to mention him.' She turned quickly to the bemused nurses. 'We must be keeping you from your work. Come on, Giselle. A quick look round and we'll be off. Oh, by the way, I nearly forgot—Ma is holding a party for all of us on Saturday evening. You'll all come, won't you?'

Without waiting for an answer, she began to show her friend around. 'There's the office——' she waved a hand '—then there's the waiting-room, the dispensary, the recovery-room et cetera. You don't need to see any more—just enough to satisfy Ma. We'd better hurry if we're going to meet Mark at twelve-thirty after we've seen the shops.' She laughed. 'Not exactly Paris, though.'

After a quick goodbye the two girls went out, leaving Lindsay and the nurses gazing at each other in amusement. At last Alison said, 'It looks as if Mark won't know what's hit him. Oh, and did you hear that bit about Giselle's cousin Pierre?'

Jessica nodded. 'It seems that Fiona is thinking along very different lines from her mother. I expect——'

'Oh, come along,' Lindsay said briskly. 'Let's stop surmising about what really doesn't concern us. I've got work to do and so have you.' She stopped. 'Goodness—I forgot. Piers asked me to ring him at Mrs Lockwood's about an imaginary emergency.' She glanced at her watch. 'Well, better late than never—he must have been there an hour ago now.'

Tapping out the number, Lindsay waited for a reply and finally heard an answering machine telling her that Mrs Lockwood was not available at the moment. She hesitated, then put the receiver down without leaving a message. The thought that Piers would be angry because she had forgotten to do as he had asked made her a little apprehensive, then she shrugged resignedly. He had probably managed to get away without any help from her. Just to make sure, she rang through to the first farm on his list. The farmer's wife said cheerfully, 'Oh, yes. He's here. Having coffee.'

The next moment he said curtly, 'You let me down, didn't you?'

She began to explain, but he cut her short.

'Don't bother. I got away early just the same.'

He rang off and, feeling rebuked, Lindsay replaced the receiver.

With difficulty she dismissed him from her thoughts and busied herself in paperwork until lunchtime. Going up to her flat, she made herself a sandwich and coffee and, sitting by the open window, she let her mind wander over the events of the morning.

So Giselle found Mark 'dishy'. Well, that was a good thing. It was to be hoped that he would fall for her as quickly as he had seemed to do in her own case. As for Piers and Fiona—well, it looked as though Denise's ambitious plans would come to naught. It was strange, she thought wryly, how parents so often were disappointed in their children's choice. Her own mother would love to have David as her son-in-law, but David was not the man Lindsay wanted. So far, she reflected, she had never met a man who made her heart beat faster. At least—with a start, she faced a recent memory—undeniably Piers had had that effect on her, but that was because. . . She paused and searched for a reason. Finally, dissatisfied, she got up to distract herself from the disturbing question to which she could find no answer. Suddenly a wave of homesickness swept over her, and with it came the guilty realisation that it was over a fortnight since she had telephoned her mother. Immediately she picked up the telephone, tapped the number and was rewarded by the sound of her mother's voice.

'Lovely to hear from you, darling. We're looking forward to seeing you as soon as your present locum engagement is up and before you go on to another one.'

Lindsay hesitated, on the point of giving the news about her newly offered permanency, then quickly decided that this was not the right moment. Much better to wait until things were more advanced. Accordingly, she promised to go down to see them as soon as she could and her mother went on to give the local news. Finally, she added, 'I nearly forgot. David is up in London. A conference or something. He'll be looking you up. Be kind to him—he misses you badly.'

A few more minutes of gossip, then Lindsay replaced the receiver and stood deep in thought. Did she want to see David? She shrugged. Obviously she would have to, but it would be difficult to find the time if he wanted to take her out. Well, she would just have to put off any invitations from Mark or Piers. She smiled mischievously. It might be a good thing to let them realise that she was not dependent on either of them for amusement. Meantime, there was this evening with Piers. The weather was still holding—it would be lovely on the river.

Back in the surgery, she had a few words with the nurses then, as they went off on their allotted tasks, she went to look in the recovery-room. She was looking at the bat when the door opened and Piers joined her.

He showed no sign of resentment at her forgetfulness with regard to getting him off the hook at Mrs Lockwood's and after they had examined the bat he said, 'I think we ought to let him go soon. That wing is healing well. The sooner he's returned to his pals the better. Sunday evening, perhaps? We must wait till dark. It's your evening off, isn't it? We could have a meal somewhere first. I know. . .' he paused '. . . come to my house. My housekeeper will lay on something for us.'

Lindsay thought quickly. If David rang, Sunday would be the only time for her to see him. She shook her head.

'I don't think I'll be free. A friend of mine is coming up to London for a conference and is going to look me up. I think I must keep that evening free for him.'

'Him?' Piers' eyebrows rose.

'Yes,' she said coolly. 'He lives near my home. A great friend.'

There was a long silence. Then he said, 'Nothing serious, I hope. Remember our agreement about entanglements.'

Lindsay's eyes flashed. 'Good grief! Do I have to undergo this inquisition every time I go out with someone you don't know? In that case——' she drew a long breath '——your offer of a permanency loses a certain amount of appeal.'

There was a moment's silence, then he shrugged. 'You call it inquisition—I maintain it's a safeguard. You must look at things from my point of view.'

'Must? *Must*?' She glared at him. 'No. You can't keep a hold on my private life.' She paused, then laughed mockingly. 'You don't believe in marriage but you're behaving like a tyrannical Victorian husband.'

His mouth twitched. 'Well, now—that's an idea! I've never pictured myself in that role. It might be quite pleasurable—especially if you were my wife.'

She choked back an unwilling laugh. It was impossible to keep up her initial fury in the face of his amusement. Contenting herself with a scornful shrug, she went back into the consulting-room and pretended to search for something in the filing cabinet.

'Lindsay——' he stood behind her '—you're not going to cancel our river picnic this evening, are you?'

For a moment she was tempted to say yes, but the prospect was too delightful to throw away.

'Of course not. I'm not so small-minded.' She turned. 'I'm looking forward to it.'

His relief was plain to see and his smile was so warm that it was impossible to stay offended. He began to speak, but was stopped by the telephone. He picked it up, listened for a moment, then handed it over. 'For you.'

Her colour rose as she recognised the caller. 'David—how nice. My mother told me you were in London—a conference, I believe.'

'It seemed a good excuse to look you up,' he said. 'It seems ages since I've seen you. I've missed you badly. Can you get away this evening? I'll come and fetch you.'

'This evening? Oh, dear.' She hesitated.

She turned towards Piers, but as though reading her thoughts he shook his head violently and muttered fiercely, 'You can't stand me up.'

'I suppose you're busy—I know the terrible hours you work.' David sounded depressed. 'I tell you what—I'll come down and wait until you've finished your evening surgery. How's that?'

'No, David, I'm not working this evening. I'm going out. Come down tomorrow.' Then she remembered. 'Oh, no, sorry. I can't manage that either. A party for the partner's daughter——'

'Look, Lindsay——' David sounded desperate '—you've got to fit me in somewhere—I'm only up here for a few days. I need to talk to you—seriously. I must know where I stand.'

Lindsay looked round cautiously, but to her relief Piers had disappeared

She said compassionately, 'David, dear, we've had all this out before. I thought I made it clear how I felt. Things haven't changed.'

'No need to rub it in. But things have changed for me. I've moved up—big promotion. Honestly, Lindsay, I could give you anything you wanted now.' He paused, but she stayed silent. He added heavily, 'I won't go back to Devon without seeing you. How about asking if you can take me with you to that party?'

She sighed helplessly. 'Sorry, David. I can't do that. But if you care to come down on Sunday, I could manage lunch with you.'

'Big deal.' His disappointment was evident. 'Well, I suppose I must be content with that.'

Replacing the receiver, Lindsay stood deep in thought. It was sad to have to be so hard with him, but it had to be done. He was certainly very difficult to shake off. Perhaps on Sunday she would be able to convince him once and for all that he was wasting his time in pursuing her. She sighed again, then, as the nurses returned, she turned her attention to work. Suddenly Alison asked, 'Are you still going out this evening?'

Lindsay raised her eyebrows. 'What makes you think otherwise?'

'Oh, nothing really, but as I came in I passed Piers and he looked like thunder. I wondered if you had had a row.'

Lindsay shook her head and was laughing it off when Jessica said, 'Someone coming in. Must be an emergency.'

The patient was a large dog of indeterminate breed, led in by an anxious woman who said, 'I know it's not surgery hours but I need to talk about Mungo. He's turned absolutely vicious. What's more, he's getting worse. His behaviour is so very strange—his character has totally changed.'

She paused. 'You'll probably think we're eccentric ourselves, because we don't believe in doctors or vets, but now—well, we can't cope with this problem. We nursed him very carefully through one illness—a friend said it was distemper—and he got over it. Then he went for a walk and chased a duck into a pond—it was a very cold day and I think he got a chill. After that he was ill again and began to turn yellow, all over—his skin, even his eyes—and we thought he was going to die. But once more we nursed him through it. Since then he seems to go mad at times. Doesn't seem to know what he's doing. For instance, today when I called him to go walkies he came out from under the table wagging his tail, then suddenly he began to growl terribly, tried to bite me and rushed back under the table. After a while he calmed down and came out, but I was very frightened.

'It's not the first time either—the other night he was in the sitting-room with me and my husband and he suddenly got up, went over to John, growling like mad, and literally tore a great bite out of his trousers. Of course, John was furious and shouted at him, and for a moment I thought Mungo was going to attack him again. His eyes were rolling dreadfully and it was only because John sat perfectly still that the dog hesitated, then went and lay down again. We decided then that we must get advice.' She paused, and looked down at Mungo with tears in her eyes. 'The worst of it is that today he seems his normal self and came with me like a lamb.'

Placed on the examination table with difficulty, the dog lay still for a few moments, then suddenly his eyes rolled and he began to struggle. With a quick sign to the nurses, a muzzle was produced and although he continued to struggle the nurses were able to restrain him. A thorough examination followed and Lindsay paid particular attention to his eyes. Looking up, she said, 'You say Mungo had distemper—wasn't he vaccinated against it?'

'He wasn't. I told you, we don't believe in those things. We've kept him perfectly healthy for three years.'

'Well,' Lindsay said carefully, 'if he'd been vaccinated, he wouldn't have had distemper. Then this yellowing of his skin and eyes—that's jaundice. He probably caught it in the pond while he was still weak. And although he seems to have survived that, his liver and his brain have been affected. I think it's too late to save him. He will get worse and very dangerous.'

'Can't you give him a vaccination, then?'

Lindsay shook her head sorrowfully and looked down pityingly at the unhappy dog. 'Too late,' she said again. 'He should be put mercifully to sleep.'

His owner gasped. 'Well, that's awful. So much for you vets! Do you mean to say that if we had had him vaccinated he wouldn't have got ill?'

'Not as badly as this, if at all. In the old days, before vaccines were brought out, dogs died in great numbers from various diseases or their after-effects. That's why owners now have to keep their vaccinations up by yearly boosters.'

His owner looked subdued. 'I'll have to ask my husband,' she said at last. 'He'll be at the office. May I ring him from here?'

'Would you like me to explain the situation to him?' Lindsay asked and, after receiving the woman's consent, she spoke to a man who was evidently relieved at her verdict.

With his mistress weeping over him, Mungo was quickly given the lethal injection and at last, after a strong cup of tea, the sad owner went home, leaving Lindsay and the nurses nearly as upset as she was.

At last, glancing at her watch, Lindsay said, 'Let's hope evening surgery won't be so traumatic. It's nearly time.'

Alison said, 'We'll take the difficult cases first and try to get finished in time for you to get away early.'

Luckily there were few people in the waiting-room and their pets were soon diagnosed and treated, but even then Lindsay realised that she was not going to have much time to get ready. Then, to her relief, Piers rang.

'No need for you to drive over to me. I'll fetch you in half an hour.'

When she opened her door to him her heart lurched.

He was so handsome, dressed in cream shorts and T-shirt, with a multi-coloured sweater flung over his broad shoulders. Then, fighting her involuntary reaction, she thought wryly, Too handsome to trust.

He in turn looked at her approvingly and as his eyes travelled downwards he grinned. 'Lovely long legs.' Looking up at her thick golden hair swinging down to her shoulders, he added, 'I think you're the most beautiful girl I've ever taken out.'

She said drily, 'That compliment depends entirely on the number of girls in question.'

He shrugged. 'Sufficient for me to be a pretty good judge. But, much as I adore beauty in a woman, it's not enough for me. Brains and character are more important. There also you come up tops.'

'I don't believe that for one moment,' she said calmly, and as they approached his car she added, 'Experience has taught me that men always go for looks. They don't really like women to have too much intelligence. It's always been the same, although men pretend otherwise.'

He stopped and stared at her. 'Your experience has obviously been most unfortunate. Has it been very— er—extensive?'

She flushed as she met his mocking gaze and said nothing. As they walked on he laughed gently. 'Well, you've answered my question. Now let's stop fighting and enjoy this glorious evening.'

Getting into his car, she said, 'You needn't have bothered to fetch me for such a short journey.'

'I wanted to make sure of you.' He grinned. 'You might have decided at the last minute not to come.'

'Well, I did turn down another invitation in favour of this.'

'Ah, yes. Your friend David. Was he very disappointed?'

'Yes, very.' She paused, then, 'He wants to marry me,' she said, and smiled inwardly as she saw his hands tighten on the steering-wheel.

His voice was suddenly harsh. 'I thought you told me you had no entanglements.'

'Neither have I,' she said calmly. 'What David wants and what I want are two different things.'

They had reached his house and as he opened the car door for her he asked, 'Is he still hoping?'

She shrugged. 'I think so, but when I see him—Sunday for lunch—I'm going to make him understand once and for all that there's no point in hoping that I'll change my mind.'

'Well, that's something. And what about Mark? I believe he's very serious about you too.'

'Who on earth told you that?' she demanded sharply.

'He makes no secret of it,' Piers said drily. 'Jim is rather pleased. He'd like you for a daughter-in-law.'

'All this talk of marriage!' She frowned. 'It's the last thing I want.'

'Is that so?' He turned to look at her as they strolled over the long lawn leading down to the river. 'Do you agree with me, then, that relationships from which one can walk away are better than being formally tied down?'

'No, I don't. You've got me quite wrong. If two people are really deeply in love, then marriage is the obvious way for them. One day I hope it will happen to me, but there's no hurry. I'm content to wait until. . .'

She paused and he said quietly, 'Until you meet this mythical deep love. Is that what you mean?'

'Yes,' she said briefly, then as the river came into view she smiled. 'Doesn't it look lovely? I'm so glad I came.'

Helping her into the boat, which was swaying gently in the current, he said softly, 'So am I.'

Making sure she was comfortable on the cushioned seat, he settled himself at the oars and pushed the skiff away from the landing-stage.

For some time no word passed between them. The only sound was the soft splash of the oars as he pulled steadily upstream. Trailing her hand in the dark green water, Lindsay watched him through half-closed eyes and revelled in the feeling of complete relaxation. She saw that he was smiling to himself at her obvious pleasure and after a while he said, 'This is a quiet stretch of the river, but further up it gets a bit busy, so I'll turn round now and find a secluded backwater for our picnic.'

She nodded dreamily and eventually he turned the skiff and pulled back against the current. The backwater he found was beautiful, overhung with leafy chestnut trees. Pink and white candles hung on boughs sweeping down, almost dipping into the water, and all around was the wild, rushy smell of the river. Steering into the bank, he shipped the oars and sat in silence as the boat swayed gently, the water lapping against the sides.

Suddenly there was a splash and a glimpse of silver as a fish rose to a hovering insect and Piers laughed.

'Well, he's got his supper—shall we have ours?' He

paused. 'Let's have it up on the bank—more comfortable for eating.'

He tied up the skiff round a strong branch and turned to help Lindsay, but she waved him aside and jumped lightly on to the grassy bank. Armed with the picnic basket and a large rug, he followed her, and at the top they settled on the edge of a meadow ablaze with golden buttercups. In the act of opening the basket he stopped.

'Listen—a cuckoo is calling from those woods over there. The evocative sound of spring.'

'I agree.' She laughed. 'I had a friend once who said he would like, in an afterlife, to come back as a cuckoo. A wonderful life, he maintained. All the fun and none of the hard work of rearing the young.' She paused and added mischievously, 'Actually he put that ambition into practice, as a lot of men do.'

Piers looked up. 'What on earth do you mean?'

'Well, he refused to get married even when his girl-friend became pregnant. He left her quite callously.'

'So lots of men do that, do they? Is that what you're saying?' Piers looked at her grimly. 'Are you getting at me? Putting me into that category?'

'Of course not!' She flushed hotly. 'I'm sorry. I didn't mean anything personal. It was just that cuckoo——' She stopped, confused, wishing she hadn't spoken so carelessly. Then, making matters worse, she added, 'It was tactless of me.'

'Got to be tactful with me, have you? Well, I assure you, I've never yet left my—er—eggs in anyone else's nest. I'm not a cuckoo—in any case, it's the female bird who does that.'

A laugh, hastily choked, escaped her and she said

unsteadily, 'I rather think this is where we ought to change the subject.'

'That's right,' he said drily. 'One should always know when to stop.' Then he grinned. 'Let's examine our picnic. I left it to Mrs Digby—my housekeeper—but I bought the wine myself. Now, what have we here?' He pulled out a plastic box. 'Cold cucumber soup— just right for this warm evening.' Once he'd poured it into bowls, they searched and found spoons and proceeded to enjoy the delicious soup. That was followed by coronation chicken, rolls and butter and then Piers said, 'Ah, yes. Of course.'

He pulled out a bottle and she exclaimed, 'Piers! Champagne! Goodness—you've gone over the top!'

He opened it skilfully and poured the foaming wine into a glass. Handing it to her, he said, 'The only drink worthy of the occasion.' He filled his own glass and held it up. 'To your beautiful eyes.'

After cheese and biscuits, they sat once more in silence. There was no breath of wind and the only sound was the continual call of the cuckoo, which brought a flickering smile to Lindsay's lips. Suddenly Piers leaned forward and stroked back a strand of her hair which was falling across her face.

'Glorious hair,' he said quietly, 'seductive eyes, a sweet inviting mouth.'

In spite of the fact that her heart was beating unevenly, she said lightly, 'Thanks for the compliments, but what I'd really like is some more champagne.'

He drew back with a rueful smile. 'I suppose I must take that as a rebuff.'

She laughed as he refilled her glass. 'You do

use some old-fashioned words—rebuff, admirers, seductive——'

'"Seductive" is not old-fashioned.' He watched her as she sipped the champagne appreciatively. 'Do you always criticise the phraseology of the compliments men pay you?'

'Of course not.' She laughed again. 'But I think you should know that flattery will get you nowhere.'

'Ah—and where do you suppose I want to get?'

She shrugged, pretending not to notice the question in his eyes. She would, she told herself, have to be very careful not to fall under the spell of this man who had such an unsettling effect on her.

Almost as though he read her mind, he said, 'You're very much on your guard against me. Am I so dangerous?'

She met his searching eyes frankly. 'If I thought you dangerous, I wouldn't be out here with you. As it is, I'm enjoying it very much.'

'More than you enjoyed yourself with Mark?'

'Much more,' she said calmly.

'And do you like me better than Mark?'

Her patience snapped. 'For goodness' sake, Piers! Don't put me through another of your inquisitions.'

He smiled at her vehemence then held out the bottle.

'Have some more.'

'No, thanks. I know when I've had enough.'

There was silence for a few minutes, then, as a bee buzzed near her face, she brushed it aside and took advantage of the diversion.

'You spoke about keeping bees the other day. I should think yours are doing well among all these buttercups.'

'No. You're wrong there. Buttercups are poisonous to honey bees. Their instinct warns them to leave them alone.'

'Good gracious.' She was genuinely interested. 'But there are quite a few around—look.' She pointed them out.

'They're making for the chestnut candles. They're on what we call tree honey at the moment—fruit blossom—apple, pear, plum et cetera. Lovely stuff. With this spell of good weather, there's what is known as a honey flow on. The bees are working like mad gathering pollen to feed the young and nectar to turn into honey.' He paused. 'I shouldn't be surprised if they swarm soon. I've warned my housekeeper to keep her eyes open and ring me immediately if that happens. I don't want to lose them as I've got an empty hive ready and waiting. If you're interested, perhaps you'd like to come and see me collect them.'

'Yes, I would. I realise now how ignorant I am about bees. It's a gap in my knowledge that I'd like to fill. Tell me more.'

He laughed. 'I'd bore you to death if I started now. It's a huge subject. But I can lend you some books containing all the latest information with wonderful photographs.'

His enthusiasm was infectious and Lindsay laughed.

'You're certainly hooked. What about getting stung?'

'Oh, that,' he shrugged. 'Protective clothing, of course, though I have often been stung. Mostly through my own carelessness.'

She pondered this for a while, then asked curiously,

'What other interests have you got—apart from veterinary work, of course?'

'Well, that takes up most of my time, but I like good
music. It relaxes me wonderfully, and so does trout
fishing, though there's not much of that round here.'

She smiled mischievously. 'I have heard——' Then
she bit her lip. Better not get too personal, she thought,
but he took her up quickly.

'You were going to say that I'm interested in pretty
girls—too interested, in fact. Well, I'm susceptible to
beauty like any other man. My ideal woman. . .' He
paused, shaking his head. 'I don't think I'd better go
into that. What about you?' He looked at her steadily.
'Have you an ideal man you dream about?'

She swallowed, realising that once more she was on
dangerous ground. He was watching her closely and
as their eyes met, suddenly, blindingly, she knew the
answer. The revelation shook her so much that her
mouth went completely dry. Knowing only that at all
costs she must not betray herself, she pretended not
to hear and brushed away an imaginary fly. He waited
and still she said nothing. Laughingly he repeated his
question and then her mind cleared and she forced
herself to speak.

'I'm sorry. I was thinking about the bees. What did
you say?'

His eyes gleamed with amusement. 'The man you'd
like to marry. Your ideal man. Have you a picture of
him in your mind?'

In full control of herself now, she threw him a mocking glance.

'Don't be silly. I grew out of that sort of dreaming
ages ago.'

He continued to gaze at her for a long moment then, abruptly, he got up.

'It's getting a bit chilly. Shall we go?'

CHAPTER FIVE

BACK at the landing-stage Piers tied up the skiff and turned to give Lindsay a hand. She smiled up at him.

'It was lovely, Piers. Thank you very much and thank your housekeeper for the sumptuous picnic.'

'Come in for a coffee—it's not late yet.' He watched her closely and when she could not hide the doubt in her face he grinned. 'You'll be quite safe. I'm not in the habit of expecting bed as payment for a nice evening.'

She flushed then laughed. 'I didn't suppose you were. But there's that party tomorrow. I'd like to get a good sleep tonight.'

'Oh, yes. The party—will you come with me?'

She hesitated. 'Well, Mark told me rather autocratically that he's going to drive me there.'

'He did, did he? At what time? Tell me and I'll come earlier.'

She frowned. 'I think I'll go with Alison and Jessica.'

'Don't be silly. They've got cars of their own.'

'I'd forgotten. Well, I'll go on my own, then. It's not as though I've got to have a partner.'

'Will you refuse to go with Mark when he comes?'

'Oh, Piers—what does it matter?' She was losing patience. 'Let me sort it out in my own way. Stop trying to arrange things for me.'

He said no more and as they walked towards his car she saw that he was frowning. Impulsively she said, 'I don't really want to go to the party. After all, I hardly know Fiona—I'm not one of her friends.'

'You'd offend Denise if you didn't go. As for Fiona—who does know her? I'm sure her parents don't understand her. She's always gone her own way and life in Paris has made her even more independent. She's got her own life there.'

Remembering Giselle's remark about her cousin Pierre, Lindsay opened her mouth to speak, then bit her lip. It was not up to her to betray what was evidently a secret. She said, 'I think Denise would like Fiona to settle down here at home.'

To her surprise Piers burst out laughing. 'Yes, and marry me. That's what Denise wants.'

'Goodness!' Lindsay turned to stare at him. 'So you know that, do you?'

They had reached his car and as he opened the door he smiled grimly. 'I'd have to be very thick not to see through Denise's scheming. Unfortunately, I can't— won't—oblige her. As I have so often said, I don't believe in marriage.'

There was nothing to say to that, but his words echoed in her mind as they drove back to her flat. When they arrived she got out quickly, but he was equally swift and as she stopped to search for her key he took her by the shoulders and turned her towards him. She stiffened momentarily as his arms folded round her, then, unable to resist, she relaxed. He lifted her face to his and she smiled up at him. It was a long kiss—tender at first, then it became more intense as his grip tightened and she lost herself in unexpected bliss. At last she pulled away and he let her go.

'Lindsay. . .' his voice lingered over her name

'. . .we must do this more often.'

She drew a long breath and said shakily, 'No, not again. This is just a thank-you kiss. Goodnight.'

He stood back and watched as she put her key into the lock then he turned back to his car. 'Sleep well,' he called, and drove away.

But sleep did not come for a long time. Finally admitting to herself that she had found the deep love she had spoken about, she wept, knowing it was doomed. No marriage—a long-lasting affair perhaps, then, when he tired of her, he would put an end to the relationship. So what was the answer? Should she throw her scruples to the wind and give herself to him, knowing it would only be a transient affair? If not, then she must try to wrench all thoughts of him from her heart.

She turned restlessly in her bed as she endeavoured to visualise a future which would inevitably end in tears. Unless—faint hope—Piers grew to love her as she loved him and abandoned his dislike of marriage. No, she told herself, that was a fantasy. He was too firmly set in his ways.

That kiss—she remembered it with a sharp pang— she had responded to it only too willingly and now he probably thought it was all plain sailing for him. Just another affair. The choice was hers. Perhaps he was right. After all, as he said, marriages nowadays so often broke down and, in the doing, caused more trauma and unhappiness than the mere breaking off of an affair to which no strings had been attached. Gradually Lindsay drifted off to sleep telling herself that she would have to leave it all to fate.

*   *   *

Saturday morning surgery was slow in commencing, thus giving time for Alison and Jessica to discuss the appropriate way to dress for the party that evening. Turning from the window, Lindsay said, 'If you go on like this, you'll never get to the party at all,' and in answer to their question as to what she was going to wear she said vaguely, 'I haven't made up my mind yet, but I don't suppose it matters much. Fiona will be the star of the evening, with Giselle a close second.'

Alison asked slyly, 'Who do you want to impress the most? Mark or Piers?'

'Neither,' Lindsay said scornfully. 'I'm just going to enjoy myself.' But even as she spoke she knew she was lying. The colour flooded into her face, and, unable to avoid the two pairs of eyes gazing at her sceptically, she tried to put them off the scent. 'Actually I'm thinking about someone who wants to marry me,' she told them, then bit her lip as the nurses seized on her words in gleeful certainty that Mark was the man concerned.

'Oh, no.' Now she could be truthful. 'You don't know him. He lives near my home in Devon. He's up in London for a few days and we're having lunch on Sunday.'

Refusing to go into more details, she was relieved when the telephone rang and cars pulled up in the yard outside. The last patient was a cat of about three years old whose owner was very worried.

'It's this terrible cough,' she said, and at that moment the large black tom gave a demonstration that was most alarming to hear. 'He's had it ever since we moved up here. We've been so busy settling in that I haven't had time to have him examined. I thought it would go eventually, but it's getting worse. The funny thing is that it doesn't seem to upset him. He eats well and looks fit, doesn't he?'

After Lindsay's examination, she asked, 'Is Timmy a hunter? Mice, birds, snails—does he eat them?'

'Oh, yes. He's never had much chance before—we lived in a second-floor flat. But our new house has fields all round and Timmy is in his element.'

'Hmm.' Lindsay sounded the cat again, then said, 'Will you leave Timmy here until this evening? I'll have to do a test to make sure, but I think he's got a lung-worm infection. It's known as Aelurstrongylus Abstruss—a minute worm which is picked up when in the larva stage from infected rodents, birds, lizards, frogs, snails.' She paused. 'It's difficult to clear up when it's advanced, as it is in this case. However, there is a treatment—granules—which deals specifically with this type of worm. If the test confirms it, when you come to pick him up I'll give you the granules, enough for five days. After that, we'll see how he is.'

With Timmy installed in a cage to await his test, they sat down to coffee and Alison said, 'What a long name for a tiny little worm. What's more, it's almost unpronounceable.'

'Well, coffee is an easy word to pronounce and that's what I hope you're going to give me,' Piers laughed as he came through the door, then, just as Jessica poured it out for him, the telephone rang. Alison picked it up, then handed it to Piers.

'Mrs Lockwood,' she said briefly and Piers groaned quietly. As he listened he frowned and they could all hear a highly agitated demand for his presence.

As he replaced the receiver Lindsay said, 'I thought

you were paying a daily visit. Haven't you been there yet?'

'No, I rang her earlier to say I couldn't make it this morning, but now she wants me urgently.'

'I'll bet she does,' Alison murmured under her breath and Lindsay shot her a warning glance.

It was too late, however, for Piers said angrily, 'I wish you girls wouldn't keep on hinting at dark goings-on with my client.' He got up. 'I'd better go. I'll try not to be too long.'

Just before he got to the door Lindsay asked, 'Why is she so agitated? What's happened?'

He shrugged. 'Her corgi bitch is whelping and she says there's something wrong. Actually, it's your work, Lindsay, but you know what she is. . .' He paused, his hand on the door-catch. 'If it's as bad as she says, it may have to have a Caesarean. In that case, I'll bring it back here for you to do.'

Lindsay gave instructions for the necessary preparations to the nurses, then went up to her flat in order to do a few chores. While she was working she reflected on the possibility of having to treat Sophie Lockwood's corgi. It was a situation she hoped would not arise, feeling it would be a test of her nerve. She was still worrying about it when the telephone rang on her extension.

Alison was almost incoherent. 'Piers has had an accident. He sounds OK but he has to go to the County Hospital. There was a lot of talking going on and I couldn't hear him very well, but I took in that he wants you to go to Mrs Lockwood in his place.'

A few minutes later, Lindsay sped along the main road, her mind full of anxiety. Then, round a bend, she came up to the scene of a bad collision between several cars and a lorry. Directed round the damaged vehicles by a policeman, she tried to see if Piers' car was there, but without success. Not knowing whether to be relieved or worried, she drove on, tense with worry, and a few minutes later was greeted by a furious look and a demand to know why she had come instead of Piers. When, at last, she was able to explain, Sophie seemed surprisingly indifferent.

'Of course I'm sorry he's been involved in an accident, but if he had come earlier he would have escaped.' She paused. 'I suppose you think I'm not sympathetic enough but my main preoccupation at the moment is with my bitch—Leonora. She's been straining such a long time. You'd better see what you can do. I shall leave you to it because I'm expecting a visitor soon.'

In the kitchen Mrs Martin looked agitated.

'I wish Mrs Lockwood wouldn't leave me to look after Leonora. But that's her all over.' She looked curiously at Lindsay. 'I thought Mr Albury was coming. Are you able to deal with a difficult whelping?'

'Of course I am.' Lindsay held back her irritation and, going down on her knees, she examined the distressed bitch. Finally she opened her case and filled a syringe.

'This injection will probably get things moving. If it doesn't, then I'll have to take her back with me and do a Caesarean.'

'Well, have a coffee, then,' said Mrs Martin, and, ignoring Lindsay's refusal, she turned, filled a mug and placed it on the table. 'I've just made it,' she said, and, obviously glad of the opportunity to gossip, went on, 'Mrs Lockwood is expecting a visit from Mr

Summers. He was here yesterday as well. I think she's rather gone on him. Your Mr Albury had better look out, if you know what I mean. Mr Summers is a widower.'

Lindsay's eyes were on the bitch and she pretended not to hear, but the housekeeper persisted.

'Don't you think that's very interesting?'

Goaded into replying, Lindsay said coldly, 'Well, no. I'm not at all interested in Mrs Lockwood's affairs.'

'Oh, that's good! "Affairs" is the right word. Well, I always say that who lives the longest will see the most. Mind you, Mr Albury himself has been cooling off lately, and I think she's fed up with trying to get him to commit himself. Now that Mr Summers has come along——'

Lindsay interrupted, her tone icy, 'I don't want to gossip about my client, so let's change the conversation.'

'Oh, if you feel like that——' The housekeeper looked offended and drank her coffee in silence. After a while she said, 'Well, nothing's happening. You'll have to take her back to your surgery and operate.'

'That's where you're wrong. Look—she's beginning to strain again.'

A few minutes later, assisted and encouraged by Lindsay, the first puppy arrived—a very large one. Lindsay laughed.

'He's the one who's been holding up the traffic.' She turned. 'Get me something to put him in, please.'

Her animosity forgotten, the housekeeper produced a cardboard carton lined with a blanket and very soon three more puppies completed the litter. After attending them and taking a final look at their mother, Lindsay said, 'I'll go and tell Mrs Lockwood that everything is OK. Four strong little puppies. I expect she'll be pleased.'

Leaving the housekeeper drooling over the new arrivals, she washed her hands and went in search of Sophie.

She found her in the sitting-room having a drink with Mr Summers, who rose as she entered and greeted her affably. Sophie, now exuding gracious charm, expressed her pleasure at the news and listened to Lindsay's instruction for the care of Leonora and her litter. Then she said, 'Mr Summers has been so helpful about my worry concerning the outbreak of EVA in his stables. I understand that now——' She stopped. 'Good gracious!' She pointed to the window. 'Look—Piers!'

As he came into the room, Lindsay felt almost faint with relief. He took the drink he was offered but Lindsay shook her head when, after a moment's hesitation, Sophie offered her one.

'No, thank you, I must get back.' She made for the door, but Piers got up quickly and followed her outside.

'I'm sorry I had to let you in for this,' he said, 'but it was a bad accident. A whole family in a small car. The ambulance took the worst cases and I drove the others—badly shocked—to the hospital.'

She nodded. 'I only heard that you had gone to the hospital and, of course, I was afraid——' She smiled tremulously. 'Thank goodness you're OK.'

He looked at her steadily for a long moment, then he said, 'Thank you for being so concerned.' He paused. 'I'll have to go and look at that mare. See you later.'

She felt so relieved that she smiled mischievously.

'According to the housekeeper you've got a rival in Mr Summers. Better look out.'

'What the hell——?' She heard him gasp as she turned away and, laughing quietly to herself, she made for her car.

As she drove along her thoughts reverted to the whelping she had successfully brought to a happy conclusion, then with a sudden start she realised that she had left her case behind. She must have left it in the sitting-room—she recalled putting it on the floor beside a large bookcase while giving Mrs Lockwood the good news about her corgi. Frowning to herself, she turned her car into reverse and drove back. Mr Summers passed her in his Land Rover coming down the drive and as she waved in return she smiled with relief. By now Piers and Mrs Lockwood would be round by the stables, which meant that she would be able to slip quietly into the house and rescue her case without being seen.

On arrival she found the main door ajar and very stealthily she made for the sitting-room. That door, too, was standing open but instead of going in she pulled up abruptly, staring in cold amazement at the sight of Piers and Sophie locked in each other's arms.

Hypnotised, she stood still for a few moments, then, recovering, she backed out into the hall. As she went towards the door she heard Sophie say brokenly, 'Oh, Piers—I thought you'd been hurt in that accident. I've tried to hide it, but I'm still in a state of shock,' and Piers murmured something indistinctly as Lindsay

continued her retreat. Closing the front door behind
her, she rang the bell and waited until the housekeeper
came. After a few words of explanation she was
ushered into the sitting-room where Piers was now
in the act of pouring out drinks. The cold look she
received from Sophie Lockwood told her how un-
welcome she was as she picked up her case, held it
up smilingly and, with a few words to explain her
return, she was out of the house in a minute.

Once on the main road she pulled into a lay-by,
turned off the engine and tried to come to terms with
the scene she had just witnessed. Sophie's hypocritical
state of shock had fooled Piers and he too was a hypo-
crite, pretending that there was nothing going on
between them. But why did he have to pretend? Why
did he make out that he was reluctant to visit her?

Lindsay sighed, a long, disillusioned sigh. It must
be that he was naturally secretive and she, Lindsay,
would be a fool to trust him. But the pain in her heart
could not be denied and hot tears burned at the back
of her eyes. She wished now that she had never come
to this practice, had never met Piers and, above all,
never had the misfortune to fall in love with him. In
an effort to console herself, she began to plan her
future. There must be no more dates with Piers, no
more talk of joining the practice; at the end of her
engagement as a locum, she would pack up and go
back home for a short break, then do more locums
until she found something permanent.

Just as she started up the car, a sudden thought came
into her mind. What about David? Married to him,
she would have a pleasant life and would be able to
run a veterinary practice from their home. Promising

herself to give the idea more thought later, she drove back to the surgery.

Engrossed in doing the test on Timmy the cat, she was joined by Alison, who said anxiously, 'I wish Jessica wasn't having this evening surgery off. We'll never be able to get away early for the party.'

Lindsay shrugged. 'We'll just have to manage. I'll be as quick as I can, but it won't matter if we're a bit late. Let's hope nothing complicated comes in.' She paused. 'Anyway, I expect I can manage on my own if necessary, so there's no need for you to stay late.'

Alison smiled gratefully. 'Well, that cat's owner will come in to fetch him so I'll just go and tidy him up. By the way, what about Dracula?'

'Oh, we're going to release him in the churchyard tomorrow evening—at least. . .' Lindsay paused and frowned. 'I think Piers will have to do it on his own. I don't expect to be free.'

As Alison went off to the recovery-room, Lindsay stood deep in thought. Much as she wanted to see the little bat returned to his kind, she knew she must not let herself in for an evening with Piers. She must be firm, she told herself, and remember how untrustworthy he was.

Then, as if to test her resistance to him, the door opened and he walked in.

She tensed up as he said approvingly, 'You did a good job with that whelping. Sophie is very grateful.' He paused. 'But what was the meaning of that last remark you shot at me when you left? About Mr Summers.'

'Oh, that,' Lindsay shrugged. 'It was more or less a joke. Mrs Lockwood's housekeeper is a terrible gossip, but obviously this time she's got things wrong. I'm sure you need have no fears on that score.'

'No fears—what on earth do you mean?' He stared. 'What are you hinting at?'

She threw discretion to the wind and said scornfully, 'Well, when I came back for my case I found the door open and walked in on a most romantic scene. So I made a quick exit, rang the bell and waited to be let in.' She paused, then added derisively, 'Poor Sophie. She was in such a state of shock—or so she said. What a good thing you were able to comfort her so adequately.'

'Lindsay!' He stared at her incredulously, his face white with anger. 'What a bitchy thing to say. I'm amazed. All I was doing was——'

'Please don't think you have to explain anything to me. I don't care what you and Sophie get up to. The only thing that makes me despise you is the way in which you pretend you don't like going to see her. Why not be honest about your affair with her? It's perfectly normal. Sophie herself makes it plain enough so why be so secretive?' She stopped, saw that he was trembling with rage, but went on regardless. 'Of course, I suppose it makes it easier for you to run several affairs at the same time.'

'Good God!' He looked so menacing that for a moment she thought he was about to strike her. Instinctively she backed away, but he seized her by the shoulders. Then, letting her go, he pulled out a chair and pushed her into it, standing over her. She closed her eyes momentarily, then heard him say, 'I don't deserve that, or your contempt.'

Looking up at last, she saw that his face was less

grim, but she got up and pushed him aside.

'I'll leave tomorrow.'

'You can't; you've still got almost two months to go as our locum.'

She shrugged disdainfully and made for the door, but he moved swiftly and barred her way.

She said, 'Well, I suppose I must fulfil the terms of my engagement, so I'll do that, then I'll leave.'

'But our offer—a future partnership—you can't chuck that away.'

'A partnership with you?' She laughed derisively. 'A man who makes absurd conditions with regard to my private life? No, that's not for me. In any case, I couldn't keep those conditions. I shall probably marry my friend David.'

He stared at her speechlessly. A muscle twitched in his temple, then he turned and went out of the room.

A few moments later Alison came back from the recovery-room and gazed at her searchingly.

'Goodness, you look a bit upset. Have you had a row with Piers? I couldn't help hearing raised voices.'

Lindsay pulled herself together and shrugged. 'We had a bit of a disagreement, that's all. Listen—is that someone in the waiting-room?'

Alison looked doubtful but went to see; she came back shaking her head. 'You're hearing things. No one there.'

With a great desire for some time alone, Lindsay said, 'I haven't had any lunch yet. I'll go up and make myself a sandwich or something.'

Alison laughed. 'Well, don't eat too much. Remember the party this evening.'

Lindsay drew in her breath sharply. 'Goodness! I'd

forgotten. Still, I need something and I expect you do too.'

'I've had lunch,' Alison grinned. 'A pot of yoghurt. I've got to watch my weight and I want to make the most of the goodies this evening.'

Her sandwich eaten, Lindsay sat brooding over a coffee. It seemed that she had come to a crossroads in her life. Would she ever come to love David as, in spite of everything, she still loved Piers? Then, as she searched her mind, a doubt crept in.

Was she mistaken? Was it perhaps infatuation that had her in a spell? The sight of him enfolding Sophie in his arms, after all that he had said about her, ought to be enough to indicate what kind of man he was. A man who could charm with flattery, whose words seemed to mean that he wanted her and whose kisses aroused her in a way she had never before experienced—that side of him had conquered her heart. But there was another side to his character that bewildered her. How could she love a man she did not understand? Or trust? That last word was the most important and one that she must keep in the forefront of her mind.

Despondently she went down to the surgery, determined to put all thoughts of love aside and concentrate on her work.

Much to Alison's relief, evening surgery was less busy than usual, but she frowned when, at the last minute, a young man walked in saying he just wanted some advice on racing pigeons. He turned to Lindsay. 'Do you know anything about them?'

She smiled. 'Well, that depends. I can give you advice on the medical side, but I couldn't tell you which bird is going to be a champion.'

'No, of course not,' he grinned. 'And it's the medical side I want advice about. I've only recently begun breeding them, and I think I've done all the right things. But I've been receiving lots of mixed advice about worming them. Some say that squabs—those are the nestlings—should be wormed, and others tell me it's not necessary. I'd like to get that sorted out.'

'Well. . .' Lindsay thought fast and to her relief she remembered the latest information on the subject. 'No,' she said decisively, 'it isn't advisable. Squabs are unlikely to need treatment until they are weaned at about three weeks old. Firstly, any worm eggs passed by the parent birds require several weeks to become infective, and a further period for development. Secondly, it's not good practice to handle breeding birds and their offspring during the rearing period unless they need medicine.' She paused. 'I suppose you know all about worming adult birds? You should do it before they pair off. And, of course, you should know all about hygiene—disinfecting and cleaning out the loft.'

The youth looked at her admiringly.

'You know your stuff, I must say. Actually, I was a bit disappointed when I saw that the vet was a woman. I didn't think you'd know the first thing about racing pigeons.'

'I like that!' Lindsay raised her eyebrows mockingly and turned to Alison. 'Male chauvinism is still alive and kicking, isn't it?'

Alison burst out laughing and the young man grinned.

'Sorry. I suppose it's the old thing about not expecting beauty and brains at the same time.'

'I think,' Lindsay said with mock-severity, 'you'd better stop before you get in any deeper.' She paused. 'Now, is that all?'

'Well, no. I'd like some worming tablets for my adult birds, please.'

Lindsay turned to the drug shelf. 'I'll give you these capsules. They're well-tolerated even at high dose-rates and won't cause feather defects.'

Suitably provided with all he needed, the youth went away, murmuring that his mates wouldn't half be surprised.

Alison laughed. 'Now if I meet any pigeon breeders I'll be able to stun them with my expert knowledge.' She glanced at her watch. 'Good grief! I'm going to be late after all. I must go.'

Upstairs in her flat, Lindsay began her preparation for the party, but all pleasant anticipation had vanished. She would have to avoid Piers and yet not allow Mark to monopolise her, though that last would be preferable.

She was just putting on her earrings when she heard a car in the yard below. Getting up to investigate, she saw Mark getting out of his Aston Martin and sighed with relief. Now she had no need to worry about avoiding Piers.

CHAPTER SIX

IT WAS not long, however, before Lindsay noticed that Mark's manner was strange. He seemed to have lost his usual exuberance. He duly admired the way she was dressed then lapsed into a somewhat uneasy silence. At last, tired of trying to make conversation, she asked, 'What's wrong? You don't seem your usual self.'

He shrugged, but said nothing, then, slowing down as they drew near to to his home, he stopped before turning into the drive. He said, 'I'm worried. I think I've made a bloody fool of myself.' He gave her a long, searching look. 'Lindsay, were you quite serious when you turned me down so firmly the other evening? Or were you just holding off for the moment and meaning to relent later on? I must know.'

She stared at him. Even in the dim light she could see that his face was drawn and his eyes were full of anxiety. This was no longer the amusing, impetuous man who had tried to storm her into marrying him.

'Of course I meant it. I wasn't leading you on. I like you very much as a friend, but there could never be anything more between us.'

She paused, expecting rather a violent reaction, but to her amazement his whole face lit up with relief.

'Oh, Lindsay, I've been a complete idiot, haven't I? I know now that I made a mad mistake.'

She laughed. 'Well, you said you were a fast worker

103

and you seem just as fast when admitting your mistake. Seriously, though, you really ought to be more cautious next time. And there will be a next time, I'm sure. One day you'll meet just the right girl for you.'

He hesitated, then very soberly he said, 'I have. Met her, I mean. And this time it's quite different. I'm not just bowled over by her looks, though she is lovely, but this goes much deeper. I know it's the real thing at last.' He paused. 'Don't laugh, please. I'm very, very serious.'

She stifled her amusement. 'I'm not going to laugh, I'm going to congratulate you. Does she know how you feel about her?'

'Well, I think she does, but I'm not rushing it. I daren't.'

Full of curiosity, Lindsay asked, 'Who is she?' then added hastily, 'I'm sorry. I shouldn't have asked that.'

'You've a perfect right to ask. You've let me off the hook so kindly.' He grinned shamefacedly. 'It's Giselle—Fiona's French friend. You've met her, haven't you?'

'Why, yes. Mark, she's lovely. What's more, when she and Fiona came to the surgery she was already taken with you. She described you as dishy.'

'Dishy!' He repeated the word slowly, then, turning, he gave her a friendly hug. 'You've made my day! Given me a bit of confidence.' He hugged her again and kissed her on the cheek. 'That's a thank-you kiss.'

She laughed and, as they separated, she realised suddenly that the car was lit up by the headlights of another one coming up behind them. It swept past into the drive and vanished round the corner where other cars were already parked.

As Mark pulled out the ignition key, he said caustically, 'Piers seems in a hurry. I suppose Fiona is the attraction. That'll please Ma.'

'You're wrong there.' Upset by the fact that Piers must have seen Mark kissing her, Lindsay forgot discretion. 'I think she's interested in someone in France—Giselle's cousin Pierre.'

'Well, it won't hurt Piers to get a bit of egg on his face.' Mark grinned. 'From what I gather, he's always had everything his own way with girls so far.'

Lindsay fell silent and Mark, preoccupied with thoughts of Giselle, made no attempt at further conversation. Soon they were in the house, made welcome by Denise and Jim and ushered into the large room overlooking the garden. Fiona and Giselle were already surrounded by several young men, most of them unknown to Lindsay, but as soon as Giselle saw Mark she left the group. The light in her eyes put a flush on Mark's face and he drew her towards the window where they stood utterly absorbed in each other.

Lindsay smiled wistfully. How marvellous to be so genuinely in love and in a world of their own, she thought. Turning away, she almost bumped into Denise.

'No drink, Lindsay? Come over here and make your choice.' Denise led the way to the end of the room. 'Ah, Piers—thank you for helping Jim with the drinks. Mark should really——' She glanced over her shoulder. 'Well, he seems to have forgotten his duty. I wonder. . .?' She glanced curiously at Lindsay. 'I thought that he and you. . .' Her voice trailed away and Lindsay smiled.

'I think he's found the real thing at last.'

Denise stared. 'He and Giselle? You think it's serious, then?'

Lindsay nodded. 'I rather think so. I'm happy for him.' She turned to Piers and said coolly, in answer to his question, 'Yes. I'd like the white, please.'

Glass in hand, she began to circulate, and soon found that she was also surrounded by various admiring men. While joking and laughing with them, she could not prevent herself from watching Piers handing out the drinks. After a while someone else took over the task and he wandered off to mix with the other guests. He made no effort to approach her and as the number of people increased she lost sight of him. The evening wore on—toasts were drunk and there was music and dancing in another room. Lindsay, invited to dance by a friend of Mark's, was on the point of accepting when a voice behind her said, 'You'll have to excuse me, but Lindsay owes me a few minutes of her company,' and the young man was left bereft as Piers led Lindsay out on to the terrace. At first she allowed him to hold her arm, then suddenly she shook him off and turned to walk back into the room.

'No.' He barred her way. 'I want to talk to you and you are going to listen.' He paused, then added, 'Come round here. I won't keep you long.'

Resentful yet curious, she went with him to a quiet corner where he pulled out a couple of garden chairs. Reluctantly she settled herself down on one, then said, glaring up at him, 'What on earth do you mean by behaving in such a cavalier fashion?'

'I'd like an explanation.' His voice was harsh. 'Mark

is obviously in love with Giselle yet you were kissing in his car before driving in. Who exactly is double-crossing whom?'

'Double-crossing! Oh! How dare you?' She flushed angrily then drew a long breath. 'You're a fine one to talk. Making up to me when all the time you and Sophie—— No!' She put up her hand as he began to speak. 'I know your kind of man. One affair after another, and sometimes two at the same time. No wonder you're so against marriage—you could never be faithful to any woman for long.'

During her furious assessment of his character he'd stood as though turned to stone. Pleased at the effect that her indignant onslaught had had on him, she got up and moved away, but an instant later he gripped her shoulders and whirled her round to face him. Unwilling to struggle, she stood rigid in his grasp, trying to ignore the uneven beat of her heart.

He said sternly, 'Now you just listen to me. I am not, repeat *not* the Casanova you think. I've had just one serious relationship and that only ended because I wouldn't consider marriage. As for Sophie—she was in a state of shock and needed comforting. You jumped to the wrong conclusion there. Now, if anyone saw us with my arms round you like this——' he pulled her against him '—what do you think they would make of such a romantic scene? But they would be quite wrong, wouldn't they?'

She said quietly, 'Just as you were when you saw Mark kissing me in his car. That was a thank-you kiss after he had told me that he was in love with Giselle and I said I understood and was glad for him. So now we're quits.'

Her anger had subsided, to be replaced by a feeling of desolation. To be held in his arms was sweet torture and for a moment she longed to confess her love for him. To her horror, she felt her mouth tremble and her eyes burn with tears. He watched her in silence until, trying to control the tremor in her voice, she said, 'I'm sorry. I think I've had too much wine. It's time I went home.'

He frowned. 'Did you take in what I said? How you have misjudged me?'

'Oh, yes. I heard what you said.'

'And you believe me?'

'Why not?' She tried to sound indifferent. 'After all, it's really none of my business. I shouldn't have berated you like that.'

He frowned, then, releasing her, he said coldly, 'I'll drive you home.'

'No need—I'll get a taxi.'

'Don't be foolish. Come and say goodbye to Denise and Jim.'

Twenty minutes later she sat beside him in his car and as he prepared to drive away he said, 'Are you feeling any better?'

'I'm not ill. There was no need to fuss.' She knew she sounded ungrateful, so, trying to make amends, she added, 'Poor Mark! He was so worried that I would be hurt because he had fallen for Giselle. He said he'd been an idiot and, of course, he had. In any case, I never took him seriously.'

'He was obviously bowled over when he first saw you. I can understand that. I was too.'

The past tense bothered her. She said bitterly, 'That's the trouble with men. They always go for looks.

And they only want one thing from women.'

She saw his hands tighten on the steering-wheel, but he said nothing. Then, as he pulled up outside her garage, he turned to look at her. She saw that his face was grim and his mouth was set in a hard line. He said coldly, 'My response to your harsh verdict is yes and no. Yes, men's sexual emotions are aroused by beautiful women—that's natural lust. And, at first, it seems as though physical possession is enough. But it never is. You spoke once of your need for a deep love—a man wants that too. A love that is both physical and spiritual. But that love is as difficult to find as water in the desert.'

Lindsay sat very still. He had put into words all that she felt for him, but his analysis of real love was so impersonal that she felt certain he had not yet experienced what he had described so accurately. At last she made to get out of the car and her hand was on the door-catch when he said, 'Is that what you feel for the man you say is going to ask you to marry him tomorrow?'

'David!' She had forgotten all about him, but now her reckless words came back to her. She could feel the blood draining from her cheeks and with the car light on she knew that Piers had seen her dismayed reaction. Ignoring the question, she pushed the door wider and stepped out on to the drive.

'So?' He looked at her quizzically. 'Have you thought up an answer to that one yet?'

She drew a long breath. 'No comment.' She paused. 'Thank you for bringing me back. I won't ask you in for coffee because I'm very tired.' Going up the steps to her flat, she took out her keys and as she opened the door she called out, 'Goodnight, Piers, and thank you again.'

As she waited for the kettle to boil, she began to undress, then, putting on a long white towelling robe, she sat down to a cup of steaming coffee. It was late, just after midnight, and the wrong thing to drink before going to bed, but she felt she needed stimulation. Her problem about David must be resolved tonight. If she was still undecided when she met him for lunch, she might well give him too much hope. Too much? Why, she mustn't give him any hope at all. He must be made to understand once and for all that she didn't love him or ever would.

She sipped her coffee reflectively. As for Piers, when he asked her about David, as he was almost sure to do, she would tell him the truth and he could make of that what he would. She sighed heavily. It was sad that she had had the misfortune to fall in love with a man whose principles were completely opposite to her own. Perhaps one day that love would fade or. . . She tried to suppress the thought that suddenly invaded her mind, but it would not go away. Finally she gave in, and faced up to an alternative that made her feel a traitor to herself. Suppose Piers asked her to enter into a relationship with him? Should she let him make love to her in the hope that one day he would change his mind and marry her?

She toyed with the idea, imagining the joy of giving herself to him with no conditions attached. That way she would find some happiness, but—and here her dream turned into a nightmare—if and when he tired of her, how degrading that would be.

Suddenly her eyes began to close and she was over-

come by a great desire for sleep. It was too big a
problem to solve. Perhaps fate would take a hand and
show her which way to go.

Next morning, with no surgeries, she was able to
get ready in plenty of time for David's arrival. She
greeted him with a smile, to which he responded with
a friendly hug. Extracting herself with difficulty, she
told him of the restaurant she had selected, and in a
short while she was seated opposite him, trying to
make conversation. After congratulating him on his
promotion, she began to talk about Devon and mutual
friends. Too late she realised that she sounded nostal-
gic and he said, 'You're homesick, aren't you? Well,
why not come back? Why not marry me and settle
down? It's a lovely part of the country and we could
have a wonderful life there. Wait——' he stopped her
from interrupting '—I've asked you so often and now
I really must have a definite answer. You've had plenty
of time to think it over. You must know your own
mind by now.'

She looked at him, saw the trouble in his steady
blue eyes and very nearly relented. Remembering the
years he had so patiently waited, always been around
when she needed someone to take her to social events
and never so much as looked at other girls, she felt
terribly guilty. If only she had never met Piers. Never
known the magnetism of his presence. Suddenly his
face rose up in her mind and she wanted to weep at the
sadness of it all. Was she making the biggest mistake of
her life? Then David reached for her hand and as he
folded her fingers in his the problem was instantly
solved. Looking down at their clasped hands, she felt
no sensation—no thrill—no warmth at all. It was a

revelation. Physically David meant nothing to her. Marriage to him could only end in disaster.

Gently she withdrew her hand and gradually, hesitatingly, she tried to make him understand. When she had finished he looked shattered and his voice was broken when he said very quietly, 'I get the message. I won't try any more.' Picking up his glass, he drained it, then pushed back his chair. 'Let's go, shall we?'

When at last they stood outside her flat he said, 'There's no reason for me to stay up here any longer, so I'll go home and lick my wounds.'

A feeling of guilt overwhelmed her, but she remained firm. 'I'm very sorry, David, but it's the best decision for both of us. Your wounds will soon heal, I promise you.'

He shrugged. 'Maybe. Meanwhile——' he reached forward and took her in his arms '—one last kiss, Lindsay. You can't deny me that.'

A few minutes later she watched him drive away, then put her key into the lock of the door of her flat. It was impossible not to feel melancholy and it was with a feeling of relief that she realised the telephone was ringing.

Her heart jumped at the sound of Piers' voice and she listened intently.

'I'm going to release the bat this evening about nine-thirty. Will you be able to come or will your—er—fiancé still be with you?'

'"Fiancé?"' She frowned. 'What on earth do you mean?'

'Well, you said——'

'Never mind what I said. You've jumped to the wrong conclusion again. David is not my fiancé. We'll never be more than good friends.'

'Good lord! I was convinced——' He stopped and she heard the unmistakable sound of a sigh of relief. Then he added, 'So you'll be free to come with me to release the bat. How about a spot of something to eat first?'

She hesitated. Somehow his invitation held no appeal. It would mean more arguing, and for the moment she had had enough.

'No, I don't think so. I have things to do.'

'Very well.' His voice was cool. 'Anyway, I'll be round at nine-thirty to collect the bat. I had a look at him this afternoon and he seems perfectly fit.'

He rang off and she stood with a hand pressed to her hot cheek. She had rejected one man who loved her, and she loved a man who despised all the principles she held dear. Suddenly she recalled her words to David. 'Your wounds will soon heal'. Perhaps she should apply that prophecy to herself. Maybe one day she would meet another man whom she could love and marry. There was plenty of time. She was only twenty-five and her career was just taking off. Far better to concentrate on that and forget about love. Independence, work she enjoyed—she could be content with that and, in so doing, she would be true to herself.

Later she went down to look at the little bat. It was still daylight, but he had been placed in a dark corner and was out of torpor. Clambering around on the bars of his cage, he looked almost desperate to get out. It was good to know that he would soon be reunited with his companions and it was to be hoped that his captivity had done no harm to his natural instincts.

The telephone rang just as she was turning away and as soon as the caller began to speak she knew she was in difficulty. A litter of terriers born yesterday needed to have their tails docked. The owner, who said he was a dog breeder, added, 'I've always done the docking myself, but with this new law I'm not allowed to. These terriers will be nearly all used for sporting purposes, so you shouldn't have any qualms about doing them.'

Stalling for time, Lindsay asked, 'You say "nearly all"—do you mean that some will be sold purely as pets?'

'Maybe a couple, but I shall keep the rest.'

She drew a long breath. 'I'm sorry, but I'm not prepared to do tail-docking. We vets are not under any compulsion either way and that is my personal choice. However, Mr Albury, my employer, may help you so I'll try to contact him. Hold the line, please.'

Hurriedly she rang through to Piers on the other line and breathed a sigh of relief when he answered. He listened, then cut her short as she began to speak of her objections.

'Tell him I'll do the tails tomorrow morning. Get his name and address, please, or are you going to refuse any help whatsoever?'

The sarcastic tone of voice made her bite her lip, but she merely said, 'Of course not,' and rang off. The client was satisfied, but Lindsay frowned as she replaced the telephone. She could see that soon they would be receiving lots of requests from frustrated breeders who had always done this job—most of them competently, but some of them deserving the ban imposed on them by the new law. It would have been easier if the law had applied to vets themselves. As it was, it seemed that there would always be a diversity of opinion on the vexed subject.

She was just going up to her flat when the phone rang again and, to her dismay, she was faced once more with the same problem. A litter of Yorkshire puppies would soon be born and the breeder wanted their tails docked within three days of birth.

Carefully she expressed her point of view then added, 'This is purely for cosmetic reasons, isn't it?'

The man said angrily that he did not expect to be put through an interrogation when he had been a client for twenty years. 'Champion dogs—I sell them all over the world. I should lose most of my customers if the dogs don't conform to the way in which they have always looked. You take off dew claws, don't you? Do a hysterectomy? Castrate difficult dogs? The whole thing about docking is completely illogical.'

Unable to refute his reasonable arguments, she calmed him down by saying she felt sure Mr Albury would do the necessary and once more rang through to Piers.

This time he said sharply, 'Mr Brown is a valued client. Do we have to lose people like that because of your trendy, ill thought out ideas?'

She said coldly, 'Well, I shan't be here much longer. No doubt you'll be able to get a more docile replacement,' and slammed down the receiver.

Fifteen minutes later, up in her flat, she heard Piers' car pull up in the yard and her heart sank. She might have known, she told herself; he was coming to quarrel with her. Well, convinced as she was of the rightness of her cause, she would fight him all the way.

Nevertheless, going down to meet him, she tensed up at the grim look on his face. He said brusquely, 'You really must compromise on the subject. I thought you'd have been convinced after the lecture Mr Harris gave you. As regards the Yorkshire terriers—docking their tails is not purely cosmetic. There is a very good hygienic reason. In breeds such as the old English sheepdog, Yorkshire terriers and Australian silky terriers, it is done to avoid fouling and retention of faeces in the perineal hairs which could lead to maggot infestation.'

Lindsay marshalled her ideas and faced him defiantly.

'Owners of those breeds should groom their animals properly and regularly to prevent such a problem. We ought to educate and train them in dog husbandry and management, rather than remove tails.'

He sighed. 'A poor argument. Firstly, how long would it take to get through to all owners that this extra work is necessary? A large percentage of dogs are ill groomed, as you know full well. And your second statement is wrong. We do not remove the entire tail. Two-thirds in the case of Yorkshire terriers, and one third for English springer spaniels.' He paused, then sat down at the surgery table and passed his hand wearily across his forehead. Slowly he added, 'We could go on like this forever. I'll admit that there is a for and against the docking business, but it doesn't seem to occur to you antis that a tremendous mountain is being made out of a very small molehill.' He stopped and looked at her hopelessly. 'Lindsay, I would never have suspected you of having a closed mind. Try to look at the argument from my point of view.'

She said frostily, 'Well, of course, you're concerned about the financial side. Your client of over twenty years might well leave you if you refuse to do what he wants. He'd probably hunt around until he found a vet who would do it—probably for a consideration.'

Piers flushed angrily. 'That is quite uncalled for. No vet would be bribed. You ought to know that.'

Succumbing suddenly to an overwhelming weariness, she said, 'Oh, let's leave it alone. You go your way and I'll go mine.'

There was a long silence, then he said evenly, 'We'll have to compromise. I'll do all the docking; you need not do any. Mind you, I myself am not in favour of doing it for purely cosmetic purposes so I'll only do it for specific breeds such as English springer spaniels being used as gun dogs in order to save them suffering from torn and bleeding tails, and other breeds for hygienic reasons. The nurses must have this explained to them and all doubtful cases must be referred to me.'

Lindsay nodded slowly. 'That seems the best way to deal with the problem.'

There was a long silence, then Piers looked at his watch. 'It will be dusk in about an hour. Time to have a quick meal. Change your mind and come back to my house. My housekeeper always leaves me more than I need.'

In spite of a sudden longing to say yes, she nevertheless shook her head.

'No, thanks. I'd rather eat in my flat.'

It sounded discourteous and she saw from his face that the snub had gone home. He shrugged. 'As you wish.' As he went towards the door he turned.

'Are you coming with me to release the bat?'

She hesitated for a moment, then said, 'Yes. I'd like that. Nine-thirty you said?'

He nodded and the door closed behind him, leaving her wondering what would have happened if she had accepted his invitation. Reluctantly she admitted that she wished she hadn't snubbed him and resolved to be more pleasant when they went together to release the bat.

CHAPTER SEVEN

BY THE time Piers arrived, Lindsay had moved the bat from the recovery cage to a smaller portable one, and as they watched the little creature all their previous differences seemed to disappear. On arrival at the church, Piers parked his car outside and, carrying the cage carefully, they walked into the churchyard.

Piers said, 'We'd better wait a while until we see where the bats are coming from.' He paused. 'Any objection to sitting here?' He indicated a large, flat tombstone and, bending down, he read the inscription. 'It's very old. Listen to this:

In memory of Thomas Stanton, Esq., who died on the third of March, 1890, and his wife, Mary Louise, who died five days later from a broken heart. In death they are happily united as they were in life for forty years.'

Piers raised his eyebrows sardonically. 'I suppose you would call that an advertisement for marriage.'

Lindsay smiled. 'Well, it is, isn't it?'

He shrugged, then, placing the bat container on the grass, he seated himself beside her and said thoughtfully, 'This is a strange place to be on a beautiful May evening.' Pointing towards the main porch, he added softly, 'Look—there's the vicar. He'll wonder what on earth we're up to.'

The tall, grey-haired man hesitated, then walked towards them as Piers rose to his feet. 'It's all right, Vicar. We're two vets here on an errand of mercy.'

The vicar looked puzzled. 'You need my help, perhaps?'

'Well, no.' Piers grinned as he told the story of the injured bat and the vicar's smile grew as he listened.

At last he said, 'Well, you've chosen a good spot to wait. In a few minutes you'll see quite a few bats emerge from just over the porch. Would you mind if I stayed to watch the release of your little patient? There's room for three on that tombstone. One of my favourites, as a matter of fact. Have you read the inscription?'

They nodded and Piers shrugged. 'The Victorians were given to flowery exaggeration. I rather doubt if this couple's marriage was as blissful as all that.'

'That's very cynical.' The vicar looked surprised. 'Don't you think it's possible to have had such a long, happy union?' He paused. 'It's not all that rare, you know. I've got several old parishioners who qualify. My wife and I are also among them.' He glanced at Lindsay and smiled. 'For a moment when I saw you two waiting here I thought you were a couple coming to discuss wedding plans with me.'

Lindsay coughed to hide her embarrassment, but Piers said, 'I wish I could look at marriage the way you do. But the statistics are against you. Nowadays, one in every three marriages breaks up.'

The vicar shrugged. 'Well, what about the other two? Why not say that two out of three marriages succeed?'

Piers laughed. 'The optimist versus the pessimist.'

'Exactly.' The vicar pointed. 'Look, here's a bat.'

A small dark shape circled round the porch for a moment then vanished in the dusk, followed by several more, and Piers prepared to release his captive. Placing the container on his knees, he turned to Lindsay. 'Would you like to open it?'

Her fingers fumbled nervously with the catch, then suddenly the cage door swung back. For a moment the bat hesitated, then like a flash he was out. He circled for a few seconds then flew off in the direction taken by the others.

Lindsay sighed with pleasure. 'That was lovely.' She turned to the vicar and laughed gently. 'I suppose you think we're exaggerating the importance of one little creature like that.'

'Not at all.' He got up. 'I think you are a charming, kind couple. Thank you for letting me share in your errand of mercy.' He smiled down at them. 'I think I'll have to find a place for it in my sermon next week. I could link it up with "not one sparrow falls to the ground" et cetera. Goodnight.'

Piers looked after him. 'There goes a lucky man. He seems to have got things sorted out.'

'All he did was to reverse your view of marriage. As for being lucky—I always mistrust that word. Luck is often another word for hard work.'

'Hard work to make a marriage last? Is that what you mean?'

She nodded. 'Yes, I think I do. All relationships have to give and take, and so often one or the other only takes.'

'Hmm.' He watched as she rose to her feet, then

as they walked back he said, 'Perhaps that's why my relationship with Penny broke up. I was the taker and not prepared to give an inch.'

Lindsay said nothing. Mixed with a pleasurable glow that he should open his heart to her was the sad realisation that he obviously regretted the break-up of his previous affair. Why, she asked herself sadly, had she imagined that he would at some time or other ask her to start a relationship with him? And why had she subsconsciously been debating whether or not to take what little happiness she could? It seemed that she had been indulging in wishful thinking. Pulling herself together, she broke the silence.

'Were you very much in love with her?'

'Oh, no. I thought I was at first, but eventually I realised my mistake.'

'Then why are you regretting it?' She knew she ought not to pursue the subject, but could not resist the desire to penetrate his mind.

He pondered the question as he waited for her to settle herself in the car. Then he laughed grimly.

'Oh, I'm not regretting it. If I'd gone along with her wishes, I would have been caught in the marriage trap with someone I didn't love. I'm really very glad it's over. Next time I'll be even more careful.'

She tried to keep the bitterness out of her voice. 'You're like most men. Any woman will do to fill your need.'

'God! That's an awful thing to say.' He turned to her before starting up the engine. 'You say I'm cynical, but that's over the top.'

Goaded by a compulsion to hurt him as he, unknowingly, had hurt her, she retorted, 'I pity the next woman who falls into your clutches. I suppose you'll make her think that you may change your mind eventually, in spite of your hang-up about marriage.'

He turned the ignition key savagely. 'It's not a hang-up, it's plain common sense.'

Her voice was cool and her heart felt even colder.

'You're really just a playboy, aren't you?' Then, as she saw him flush angrily, she added, 'Let's change the conversation. There must be other things to talk about.'

He was breathing fast, but he shrugged and said, 'As you wish,' then stayed silent until he pulled up outside her flat. Watching her as she got out of the car, he said calmly, 'Aren't you going to ask me in for coffee?' She turned to stare at him and he stared back mockingly. 'It's all right. I'm not going to try anything on. I know I wouldn't get very far. You'd tear me to pieces with that sharp tongue of yours.'

She passed that off with a scornful laugh, but her heart felt like lead. Going up the steps, she put her key into the lock and turned to look down at him. 'Goodnight,' she said, and saw him lift his shoulders carelessly as he turned the car round and drove away.

Alone, she faced up to reality. He was selfish to the core. A self-confessed taker, not a giver. Pacing her room, she mourned the fact that she could not love David. But then if she married him she in her turn would be a taker like Piers. Despondently she prepared for bed and just before going to sleep she made another resolve to avoid going out with him again.

That resolve was put to the test again when, next day, Piers came in after his morning calls and joined

them for coffee in the surgery. They were just finishing
when a call came through from his house. He listened,
said, 'I'll be right over,' and grinned as he replaced
the receiver. Getting up, he said, 'My bees are swarming and my housekeeper is in a state of near panic,
rushing round and shutting all the windows and
doors.' He glanced at Lindsay. 'You said you would
like to learn about bees. Well, now's your chance.
Come with me and see what happens when they
swarm.'

With no operations to do, she could not find an
excuse. As they walked out to his car he said, 'This is
a perfect morning from the bees' point of view. Warm,
no wind, no rain—a great day for their one holiday
of the year. I just hope they'll settle in an easily get-at-
able place. Mrs Digby said they were pouring out of
the hive, so let's hope it's a big swarm.'

Lindsay felt a little apprehensive. 'Are we likely to
get stung?'

'Oh, no. They almost never sting while swarming.
They can often be handled without any protective
clothing. One view of this is that while preparing to
swarm they fill themselves with as much honey as they
can carry to last them for several days.'

As soon as he'd pulled up in his driveway they got
out and he led her down to where his three hives stood.
To her surprise, all seemed normal and Piers stood
contemplating for a few moments. Then he said, 'Mrs
Digby didn't watch to see which direction the swarm
took, so we'll just have to search. Sometimes they fly
for quite a distance. Let's—oh, yes—look! There they
are. On a branch of that plum tree.'

For a moment Lindsay couldn't see anything

unusual, then she noticed a few bees flying around a great vibrating mass which was rapidly increasing in size.

Piers said, 'I'll just wait for them to settle. If the queen is there they won't take long. I wish we could have been here when they left the hive. It's a wonderful sight. They stream out and swirl upwards, dancing in the sunshine, full of excitement on this one and only play day. There is a sort of roar—the music of the swarm—it's lovely to hear.'

Lindsay found herself caught up in his enthusiasm and stared fascinated at the heap of golden insects.

'It's so mysterious,' she said. 'They seem to know exactly what they're doing. Yet you say it's all instinct.'

'Yes. That's how they survive.' He paused. 'Strange to think that bees were on earth long before man arrived.'

'How do you know that?'

'Fossils from prehistory sometimes contain ancient bees in a perfect state of preservation. When flowering plants arrived in the Mesogic Era, bees appeared to fertilise them.' He turned away. 'I'll just go and get a skep to put them in.'

He returned with a round straw skep plus a large hat with veil and gloves and Lindsay laughed at his appearance as he put them on. He said, 'Well, I don't believe in taking chances, although I'm almost sure there's no real need with a swarm.'

He placed the skep immediately underneath the hanging mass and gave the branch a firm, sharp blow. A few bees flew out wildly, but the bulk of the swarm fell like a great sponge into the basket. Quickly he turned it upside-down, then, picking up a piece of brick, he propped the skep up on one side. He said, 'If the queen is there, as I think she is, they will form into another mass, hanging from the roof. If, by any chance, she isn't with them, then they'll all come out in search of her.' He stood watching closely. 'Ah, she must be there. They're staying in. Come and see.'

She went forward cautiously. Fascinated, she stared in silence then, turning to Piers, she asked, 'What are those bees doing? They're acting in a strange kind of way.' She pointed to a little group, about half a dozen, who had come out on to the edge of the skip and were standing on their front legs with their ends up in the air.

'They're opening up the scent glands in their tails and fanning furiously with their wings to guide all the stragglers to their new location.' Piers laughed, obviously pleased at Lindsay's interest. 'There's no end to the wonderful things they do. I could go on forever about the facts that have been discovered over the years, but I'm afraid I'd bore you to death.'

She shook her head. 'I'm certainly not bored. I'm completely hooked.'

He smiled. 'Well, there are masses of legends about them, of course. One, for instance, says that, when they die, bees alone among the insects go to heaven. Another folk belief is that immorality on the part of the beekeeper will result in arousing the bees to stinging fury. In some places it was the custom of young girls to test their suitors by leading them past a hive of bees.'

Lindsay stifled a laugh and bit her lip in order to hold back the obvious retort.

He grinned. 'I can read your mind. You're thinking that if girls did that today I'd probably be stung to death.'

She laughed. 'Something like that.'

He shook his head and laughed mockingly. 'Actually, I hardly ever get stung, believe it or not.' He looked at his watch. 'I must go, but I'll be back this evening to put them into the new hive.'

'Won't they fly away meantime?'

'No. They'll be anxious to stay under cover.' He paused. 'Will you come to watch? That is, if you're really not bored.'

She shook her head. 'I'm very interested. I'll certainly come if I can. Directly after evening surgery, if that's not too late.'

'Just come as soon as you can. It won't be dark till about nine-thirty.'

'Suppose you can't make it—say, an urgent call keeping you out till after dark. What would happen then?'

'Well, a swarm won't fly after dark. They'll be OK.'

Walking back, Lindsay said thoughtfully, 'I suppose a knowledge of bees might be helpful to a vet. They get certain diseases, don't they?'

'Yes and there's a new disease—well, new to this country. It's called Varroasis. A parasitic mite, simply called Varroa. It's spreading and will eventually spread to every apiary. Infested colonies die if left untreated. I've got a leaflet from the Ministry of Agriculture telling beekeepers what to do. There's a lot of work involved.' He paused, his mouth twitching. 'Does that soothe your conscience?'

'What on earth——?' She stopped in her tracks and stared at him in bewilderment.

He gazed back at her steadily. 'Well, now you can tell yourself that this association with me is purely in the interests of science. Which it is.' He paused, watching her colour rise, then added drily, 'Of course, I naturally prefer to think that you take as much pleasure in my company as you do in the bees.'

She looked away. There was, she thought bitterly, nothing to say. His words were sweet to hear, but they were only words, with no depth to them. For one wild moment she wondered how he would react if she told him that every moment she spent with him filled her with longing to be held in his arms. As it was, she thanked him calmly and promised to be on time after evening surgery.

Luckily, there were not too many people in the waiting-room that evening and most of the cases were routine. Cats and dogs followed in quick succession. Injections were given, antibiotics were prescribed and appointments for operations were made. There was one upsetting incident, when a cat in the last stages of acute renal failure died on the table, and Lindsay was about to tell the owner that he should have brought his pet in sooner, but, on seeing the genuine grief in the old man's face, she did her best to comfort him instead. When the door closed behind him Jessica asked, 'Could you have saved him if he'd come in sooner?'

'Well, when the symptoms showed—losing weight, increased thirst, intermittent vomiting—I would have done tests, treated him accordingly and put him on a specially balanced diet that would at least have lengthened his life. But Mr Jones had been treating him with all kinds of quack remedies which promised everything but actually did more harm than good.' She sighed. 'Well, there it is. Is that the last patient?'

Alison looked pleased. 'No more in the waiting-room. We're actually going to get away on time for once.' She turned to Lindsay. 'Have a good time with those bees. Not my idea of a romantic evening, but perhaps if you get stung Piers will comfort you in his own inimitable way.'

Lindsay stared. 'Alison—how is it you know everything that goes on round here?'

'It's a gift.' Alison grinned mischievously. 'Actually my mother knows Mrs Digby—Piers' housekeeper. There's not much that escapes her.'

'Well, gossips usually exaggerate everything.' Lindsay tried to control her irritation. 'There's no question of romance. I'm anxious to learn about bees. So pass that on.'

Her irritation increased as Alison muttered something about onlookers seeing most of the game, then made a quick get-away before Lindsay could find an adequate retort. Meeting Jessica's sympathetic gaze, she shrugged resignedly.

'I shouldn't have given her the chance to talk such nonsense.'

'Oh, Alison reads romance into everything,' Jessica said easily, 'and she's usually wrong.'

But the gossip had its effect and on arrival at Piers' house Lindsay looked carefully at the housekeeper when she opened the door. After saying that Mr Albury was down with the bees, Mrs Digby added, 'I'm going home soon, but I've left dinner for two ready as Mr Albury asked me. I hope you enjoy it.'

Once out of sight of the house, Lindsay stood still, deep in thought. Perhaps it would be best to abandon all interest in the bees. And Mrs Digby would be deprived of gossip when next day she saw that Piers had eaten alone. Undecided, she put the thought to the back of her mind and went on to join him by the beehive.

His face lit up when he saw her and, as always, her heart gave an uncontrollable leap. Then, reminding herself that this was an educational exercise, she asked, 'How are you going to get them into their new home?'

'Well, there are various methods, but this is the way I do things. Over there, outside the empty hive, I've put a board at an angle to the ground, making a run-up to the entrance. I've draped a small white sheet over the board and on to the ground. Now watch—I'm going to lift up the skep and tip the swarm on to the sheet.'

He picked it up and carried it to the empty hive, while Lindsay drew back rather apprehensively.

He shook his head and laughed.

'No need to be nervous. Come and help me watch for the queen. It will be easy to pick her out on the white sheet.'

In one swift movement he tipped the mass of bees on to the sheet, then stood watching.

'See——' he pointed '—a few bees are running up the slope. They're going to inspect the hive to find out if it's suitable.'

A few moments later they came out, returned to the main body and then the swarm began to climb up the slope to the hive.

'Now for the queen,' Piers said. 'She's much bigger than the others—a good inch in length with reddish-coloured legs.' He waited, then suddenly he said, 'There she is. See?'

Lindsay leant forward and gasped.

'Goodness! She's unmistakable. I can't believe it! Do you know, this is the first time I've ever seen a queen bee? I must say I find all this terribly interesting.'

Obviously pleased at her reaction, he said, 'Well, this is only a very small part of bee-keeping. Come into the house as soon as I've finished and I'll pick out a book on the subject for you. I'll be about half an hour.'

Without thinking Lindsay said, 'Yes. I'd like to learn more,' then bit her lip as she remembered that dinner laid for two. She was no queen bee to be lured into a carefully prepared trap. She said ruefully, 'Half an hour? Oh, I don't think I can spare any more time after that. Perhaps you could look out a book and let me have it tomorrow in the surgery?'

He hesitated. 'Well, now that the queen is in there's really no need to wait. I can come back later and see to them.' He paused. 'Why are you in such a hurry to get away? No calls have come in on my mobile phone.'

'Oh, it's not that. Just things to do in my flat.'

'They can wait, surely? I was hoping that you might stay and have a spot of something to eat. Mrs Digby always leaves too much for me.'

Laughing inwardly, Lindsay said drily, 'Mrs Digby

told me she had left a meal for two as instructed by you. She hoped I would enjoy it.'

'Oh, dear!' Piers laughed ruefully. 'What a give-away. I thought it would be better to ask you casually. As a vet, you know, it's better to be slow and gentle with a nervous patient.'

'Nervous patient indeed! Is that what I am? A kind of neurotic pet?'

'No, no, of course not!' The laughter left his eyes and he gazed at her steadily. 'An unfortunate metaphor. Nevertheless, I mean it when I say I don't want to rush you into anything.'

'Rush me into what?'

'You know very well what I mean. I'm sure you've received many such invitations. Why, for instance, did you go out with Mark when you knew he was making a play for you?'

Unable to explain, she said evasively, 'Are you making a play for me too?'

'Of course I am,' he said blandly. 'You're so beautiful and, above all, so—well, interesting, that any normal male would want to know you better.'

'I think you know me well enough by now. Just as I've come to know you.'

'You're wrong,' he said firmly. 'We know each other as vets, yes. But I don't pretend to understand you properly. Come on, Lindsay—a meal on the terrace on this lovely May evening. Keep me company—I'm quite lonely, you know.'

'Lonely men are usually dangerous, but—oh, well— I'll take pity on you.'

He smiled down at her and her heart seemed to turn over with love, but as he put his arm round her shoulders she drew back and shook her head.

'We're just friends, remember?'

'God!' He withdrew his arm. 'You can't be as cold as you pretend.'

'I'm not pretending. I just don't want you to think I'm——' she searched for the word '—well, available.'

She saw him wince, but he said no more. It was not until they had nearly finished the delicious salad laid out for them and were drinking the last of their wine that he broached the subject again. Leaning forward, he asked, Lindsay, what do you mean by not being available?'

'Oh, goodness!' She pushed her empty plate aside impatiently. 'Don't pretend you don't know.'

'I'm not pretending. I just want you to explain exactly what you mean.' He paused, then added quietly, 'Do you care for me at all, Lindsay?'

The colour rushed to her face, then, as she met his eyes, she said, 'I like you, but I don't like the way you look at life.'

'My morals, you mean?'

She nodded. 'Old-fashioned, aren't I?'

'Yes, very.' His expression was hard to read, but it made her feel she was priggish and intolerant. She thought unhappily, I suppose I am, but I'm not going to tell him that I almost hate myself for not being more liberated. Nor must I let him know that he is the only man who could make me change my mind, because if he began to make love to me I'd be lost.

He seemed, as always, to read her thoughts. He said slowly, 'I wonder if I could make you come round to my point of view?' Suddenly he got up, put his hands on her shoulders and looked deeply into her eyes. 'Would a kiss do it?'

'No,' she said vehemently. Shaking him off, she added fiercely, 'Don't play with me like this. Say what you want and I'll give you a straight answer.'

He was silent and she endeavoured to pull herself together so that she could stand firm against the temptation that was pulling her towards him.

At last he said calmly, 'I want to know if you'll let me make love to you.'

Her eyes filled with hot tears, but she controlled her voice.

'Just get this straight, Piers. I don't want your kind of love-affair—easy come and easy go. Find someone else to sleep with.'

His face whitened and he said grimly, 'Well, that's a straight answer. A definite rejection.'

Holding back the tears, she got up to leave and he watched her silently. Then suddenly he asked almost angrily, 'If I asked you to marry me, would you say yes?'

She stared at him incredulously. 'Marry you? Just like that? But you don't love me—you only want——'

'Of course I want you, and if marriage is the only way in which I can have you then marriage is what I'm offering.'

Now the tears won over her self-control and, blinking them back, she exclaimed, 'That's horrible!' Her voice broke. 'Piers—how can you? You're making it sound as though I'm bargaining with you.' She tried to sweep her tears away and he reached forward as though to take her into his arms, but she burst out again, 'Don't touch me. You're hateful. Utterly cynical. What kind of marriage would that be? Just legalised lust! How long would it last? Two years? A year? More likely only a few months.'

She saw even through her tears that his eyes were blazing with fury, but he made no attempt to stop her as she rushed past him without another word.

CHAPTER EIGHT

STILL smarting from the events of the evening before, Lindsay was talking on the telephone when, next morning, Piers walked into the surgery. Putting her hand over the receiver, she turned and said coldly, 'Mrs Lockwood wants me to go over there and dock the puppies' tails. I'm trying to make her understand that I don't do that, but——' she shrugged '—perhaps you'd better deal with her.'

He grimaced as he took the receiver and there was silence in the surgery as Lindsay and the two nurses waited expectantly. For a whole minute Piers said nothing, but they could all hear Mrs Lockwood's voice rising indignantly. At last he said quietly, 'Sophie, you know very well what the situation is. I explained it fully the other day. You agreed at the time. Why have you changed your mind?' He paused, listened, then went on, 'Two of your buyers only want tail-docked dogs? Well, they're going to be unlucky. There is no reason for docking corgi tails—they're not going to be used for sporting purposes.' He paused, then nodded. 'Very well, I'll ask Lindsay to take off their dew claws. I'll hand you over to her.'

Passing over the receiver, he gave a sigh of relief, and sat down to drink his coffee. After fixing an appointment, Lindsay came back to the table and Piers said, 'I have to go to Mr Williams—the EVA case. Would you like to drop in and see how things are

136

progressing? After you've done the dew claws.'

She shook her head. 'Thanks, but no. I've lots of things to do here.' Then, to stop him asking just what those things were, she added, 'What's happening to the EVA case? Has the infection spread to the other horses?'

'No. Mr Williams has managed to keep the mare completely isolated. I think the disease been contained. And Sophie's mare hasn't contracted it, though, of course, she's still very nervous.' He paused and smiled. 'She and Mr Williams are great buddies now and he does his best to allay her fears. Now——' he got up '—how about meeting for lunch? There's a very good pub just near Sophie's place—the Black Dragon.'

Lindsay shook her head again. 'I told you, I have a lot to do. I must come straight back here.'

'Well, you've got to have lunch somewhere,' he persisted, then turned to the nurses. 'You'll know where to find me if necessary.'

As the door closed behind him Alison said, 'I thought everything here was well under control. What have you got to do that we can't?'

Lindsay shrugged. 'I've always got something to do up in my flat.' Avoiding Alison's sceptical smile, she picked up her case. 'I'm off to Mrs Lockwood now. See you later.'

On her way she fell to wondering why Mrs Lockwood had asked her to take off the puppies' dew claws. Perhaps she hoped she would be able to overcome Lindsay's objection about the tail-docking. On arrival she found her guess was correct, for as soon as the dew claws were removed and the puppies returned to their mother Sophie turned on the charm.

'I know you don't agree with tail-docking, but surely just this once. . .? I'll make it well worth your while.'

Furious at the hint of bribery, Lindsay picked up her case and made for the door. The other woman's eyes blazed with anger as she snapped, 'So I'll have to shop around for a vet who isn't as disobliging as you are. I'm pretty sure I'll find one.'

'In that case, you won't be wanting me any more,' Lindsay said calmly. 'If you do find a vet who will do the tails, he or she will naturally expect to do all your work in future.'

'Why, you arrogant little——'

Mrs Lockwood broke off suddenly and, following her startled gaze, Lindsay turned to the window and saw Piers and Mr Williams coming up the path. She said quickly, 'I can see myself out. Goodbye.'

If she had hoped to get into her car before the arrival of the two men she was unlucky. Mr Williams greeted her in a friendly fashion, then strolled on, but Piers stopped.

'You look angry. What's the matter?'

Lindsay hesitated, then shrugged. 'Mrs Lockwood tried to bribe me to do the tails, then lost her temper when she didn't succeed.' She paused, then added scornfully, 'She'll probably work her charm on you and wind you round her little finger.'

'Come off it, Lindsay. Don't take your temper out on me.'

She drew a long breath. 'Anyway, she's going to try another vet so if she finds one you'll have lost a valuable client.'

To her surprise, he laughed. 'A good job too. I couldn't care less. Now, Lindsay, change your mind and have lunch with me. I only came here with Williams in the hope of catching you before you left.'

She could feel herself weakening, but was saved by the appearance of Mrs Lockwood, who was standing on the steps. She called loudly, 'Piers, I'd like you to have a look at Cora to make sure the urticaria hasn't come back.'

Lindsay started up her car while Piers muttered something under his breath then he said quickly, 'The Black Dragon—half a mile up the road on the right. Wait for me there—I won't be long.'

She shook her head, but he had turned away and she frowned, torn between a wish to do as he said and a resolution to avoid any friendly intimacy. A few minutes later she pulled up outside the pub and sat still, trying to make up her mind. At last she restarted the engine. Much as she wanted to be with him, she knew that only professionally could there be any link between them. The trouble was that every time he spoke to her, each time their eyes met she yearned for him and she was always afraid that her feelings would betray her. What puzzled her was that he seemed to seek her company no matter how curt she was to him, no matter how angry he had been. Perhaps he thought their quarrels were of no importance. She nodded to herself. That must be the reason. Maybe it would be a good idea to copy him and treat each disagreeable episode as something too trivial to bother about.

On entering the surgery she was met with the sight of Jessica and Alison in consultation with a young man who turned to her and said, 'Remember me? The pigeon breeder?' He pointed to what appeared to be a dead pigeon on the table. 'I've got another problem for you.'

She asked anxiously, 'Has this bird just died?'

'He's four months old and I found him dead this morning. I'd like you to find out why. He hasn't been shot, I've examined him for that, so I'm wondering if he's been poisoned or died of some infection. I'm worried that it might be something that could spread to the other birds.'

'He's very thin.' Lindsay picked the small body up. 'Obviously hasn't eaten lately. I think the only way to find out is by doing a post-mortem. Is that all right with you?'

The young man nodded. 'May I stay and watch? I'm not the squeamish type.'

It didn't take long to solve the mystery. Opening the bird's gizzard, she looked into it closely, then with a pair of forceps she pulled something out and said, 'There you are.'

'A nail! Good lord!' The youth stared. 'Where on earth——?' He paused, then frowned. 'I wonder——? Yes, that must be it. I've been doing some repairs to the woodwork of the loft and I must have dropped the nail in the corn grains lying around. Who would have thought——?' He shook his head ruefully.

Lindsay said, 'You'd better make sure there aren't any more nails lying around or you'll have more trouble.' She smiled. 'That was just about the quickest PM I've ever done.'

When the youth had gone, Lindsay turned to the nurses. 'I'm a bit hungry so I'll just go up to my flat and make myself a quick sandwich.'

Alison looked at her curiously. 'We thought you

were having lunch with Piers. He rang through to say we could get you at the Black Dragon.'

'I changed my mind,' Lindsay said shortly, and frowned as Alison groaned.

'Oh, no! Not another quarrel. I can't under-stand——'

'There's nothing to understand. I'd already said I didn't want to go to the pub, but you know Piers—he takes too much for granted.'

The nurses glanced at each other and Jessica said, 'We don't know Piers as well as you do, but we do know that he seems fascinated by you and we have the feeling that you're playing hot and cold with him. All right——' she shrugged '—you needn't glare at us. It's an intriguing situation that brightens up our rather boring lives.'

Lindsay's self-control snapped. 'Well, you'd better find some other form of entertainment. There is no "situation" between Piers and me, so you'd better stop fantasising about us.'

Her back was towards the door and it was only when she saw Jessica's horrified gaze that she turned sharply. Piers stood in the doorway, his eyebrows raised in amusement. Speechless, Lindsay stared at him, quel-ling with difficulty an impulsive desire to run into the office and shut the door behind her. Instead she indi-cated a few pigeon feathers on the table and said calmly, 'I've just done a PM on a pigeon. A nail in its gizzard. That's a bit unusual, isn't it?'

His eyes mocked her. 'Yes, it is unusual, but life is full of surprises.'

Alison giggled and Jessica coughed with embarrass-ment as he passed them and went into the office. Over his shoulder he said, 'Lindsay, would you mind coming in here for a moment?'

Shutting the door behind her, he said evenly, 'What's all this? Are those girls gossiping about us?'

She nodded. 'Yes. They're being very silly. However, I think I've managed to make them see sense.'

'I suppose it's inevitable, but I find it irritating. . .' He paused, then gave a short laugh. 'So they think you're playing hot and cold with me. More cold than hot, I should say.'

'How long did you stand there eavesdropping?' Lindsay asked indignantly.

He laughed again. 'I heard my name as I came into the passage and was curious enough to stand still for a moment. Well, they say that eavesdroppers hear no good of themselves, so it serves me right. Let's forget it. Now, why didn't you wait for me at the pub?'

'I never said I would.'

'True.' He nodded amiably. 'All the same, I was hoping for a talk with you. Let's have it now.'

She shook her head. 'I'm just going to make a sandwich. It'll have to wait till later.'

'No,' he said emphatically. 'It can't . Look, I'm hungry—I didn't go into the pub when I saw your car wasn't there. How about making two sandwiches and two coffees?'

'What—up in my flat?'

'Why not?' His mouth twitched. 'Give the girls something really interesting to talk about.'

'That would be quite idiotic,' she snapped, but he grinned.

'I'll deal with them.' He reached for the door-handle. 'Up you go and start cutting the sandwiches.'

Before she could stop him, he opened the door and ushered her out and as she went upstairs she heard him say, 'Lindsay and I will be up in her flat having a snack. Make of that what you will, but don't get too carried away by your fertile imaginations. We just happen to be hungry.'

As the door closed, Piers said, 'That's set them off all right. Just listen to that hysterical laughter.'

Lindsay pursed her lips, wondering if Piers hadn't made matters worse, but there was nothing she could do about it. Resolved to put a quick end to his visit, she set about cutting sandwiches and making coffee so fast that he looked at his watch as she came out of the kitchen carrying a tray.

'Good lord! That didn't take long. You must be very anxious to get rid of me.'

This was too near the truth to be comfortable and Lindsay flushed as she handed him a plate. She said quickly, 'I'm anxious to hear what you want to talk about. Is it something to do with Jim's offer of a partnership? Because if——'

'No, it's quite different. It's—well, I'm going to ask you to do me a favour. Will you?'

She stared at him in surprise. 'Well, that depends, doesn't it?'

He hesitated, as though unable to find the right words. At last he said, 'My aunt Phoebe is coming up to London for a few days' shopping. She'll be staying with an old friend. Then on Sunday she's coming down here to see me and I'll be taking her out to lunch.'

'That's nice for you, but what has that to do with me?'

'It's like this. My aunt will be bringing her friend's

daughter with her and I want to ask you if you'll join us for lunch to make up a foursome.'

She frowned. There was something strange about this invitation. 'Surely, Piers, I'll be out of place? I'd feel very awkward.'

'No, you wouldn't. I have a very good reason for asking you.' He stopped and she waited, her curiosity aroused by his diffident manner. He said slowly, 'I'd like you to meet my aunt.'

She looked at him steadily. 'There's more to it than that.'

He grinned. 'Very perceptive of you. I'd better come clean. This friend of my aunt's is a girl I know very well. She lives near my old home and we went around together for a while. Rather like you did with your David. The trouble is, my father is very keen for me to marry and my aunt thinks this girl is the right one for me. I just thought it would be a good idea to cool the situation by bringing you along.'

Lindsay froze. She said coldly, 'So am I supposed to be the girlfriend of the moment?'

He nodded, his mouth twitching. 'That's the general idea.' He paused. 'No need to look so disapproving. There's nothing much to it. I just want them to realise that Katie isn't the only girl in the world.'

'Piers, what a low-down scheme! I didn't ask you to help me out with David. I was firm and he accepted my decision. This poor girl—is she in love with you?'

'Certainly not, but my aunt is trying to brain-wash her.'

In spite of herself Lindsay laughed. 'Your aunt must be a bit of a dragon.'

'Far from it. She's very gentle and kind. I love her—

she practically brought me up. My mother left my father when I was four. When I was six, my aunt's marriage also broke up and she came to live with us and look after me.' He paused. 'She made a good job of it, too, but I'm not a small boy now and she must realise that.'

Lindsay nodded. 'I can understand that. All the same——' Suddenly an alarm bell rang in her brain and she said, 'You know, Piers, I don't think you're being quite frank with me. You want me to put on an act for you and I don't like that at all. What's more, you've done this before. At least, that's what Alison said when you took me to Mrs Lockwood's for the first time. Is this the method you use to shake off a girl when you find she's beginning to think of you as a possible husband?'

He flushed. 'It lets them down gently.'

'Well, count me out!' Lindsay glared at him. 'You can find yourself another girl to act as a shield for you. Take Alison or Jessica.'

'Don't be stupid. They're not my type at all.'

'Neither am I.' She got up and looked down at him scornfully. 'If you've finished your coffee, you'd better go.'

'But you're wrong. You are my type, Lindsay.' He rose and moved towards her. Automatically she retreated a few steps. He said, 'It's all right. I'm not going to kiss you. I've got enough strength to resist you, though I'm getting weaker all the time. It's OK. I won't bother you again. Forget the whole thing, please.'

Evening surgery was very busy. The spell of unusually warm weather was bringing the usual problems. Eczema cases predominated and some were treated with injections and others with antibiotic ointments. A spaniel was brought in shaking his head violently and examined with an auroscope which showed up a grass seed deep down in the ear. Lindsay endeavoured to get it out with forceps, but eventually she shook her head. 'It's too far down. I'll put some olive oil in to soothe the ear through the night, but I'll have to give him a general anaesthetic in the morning.' Another patient had a tumour to be removed and two cats to be spayed were added to the morning list.

'It looks as if we're going to have a busy surgery tomorrow,' she said as the last patient left. 'I just hope there won't be any late calls. I don't like being tired when I operate.'

But at ten o'clock that evening there was an urgent call.

'Greenford here.' The farmer was obviously agitated. 'Three of my cows are out—well, we've just got two back, but the other one wandered on to the main road. It's been hit by a car. Badly injured—think it'll have to be put down. You can't miss it—just by the entrance to our lane.'

He rang off before she could ask any questions and left her hesitating. This was obviously a job for Piers and, her decision made, she rang through to him. He was instantly alert and was about to ring off when she said quickly, 'I'll come with you. I might be able to help.'

He hesitated for a moment, then said, 'Well, OK; I'll pick you up.'

She waited for him outside, and, getting into his car,

she asked, 'Have you got your humane killer?'

'Of course. I hope it won't be necessary but Mr Greenford is probably right. I wonder how those cows got out? Greenford will have to bear the responsibility. I wonder if the driver of the car is hurt?' He paused. 'There they are—see those lights.'

A car, its bonnet smashed in, had been pushed over to the side of the road and several men were standing around looking helplessly at a large cow lying very still in a hunched-up position. A police car had drawn up and one of the two officers was directing approaching traffic. A gloomy Mr Greenford greeted them.

'One of my best milkers. Both front legs broken, I'm fairly sure. You'll have to put her down.'

'I'll just make sure.' Piers handed the humane killer to Lindsay, then bent down to the unfortunate animal, who groaned pitifully as soon as he gently lifted a leg and felt it carefully. He nodded, looked at the other leg and turned to Mr Greenford.

'You're right. Poor creature.'

'Poor me, you mean. I can't imagine how much this is going to cost me. I might get some help from my insurance, but——' He lifted his shoulders helplessly and pointed to the damaged car. 'That too,' he said.

'What about the driver?' Piers took the humane killer from Lindsay.

'He's been taken to the hospital. Badly shocked. He'll be all right. And all because a gate was left open.' The farmer glared at three of his men standing by a tractor with a large trailer attached. 'Nobody's owned up, of course, but I'll find out eventually. Ultimately it's my responsibility, of course.'

'I'm afraid it is, sir.' A policeman was standing by.

'An animal loose on the highway is always the responsibility of the owner.'

Mr Greenford nodded impatiently, then turned to Piers and glanced at the humane killer.

'Are you going to do it here?'

'Yes, of course,' Piers said sharply. 'That cow is in no state to be lifted on to your trailer. She'd go through agonies of pain.'

The farmer frowned. 'I was wondering if we could get her to the knacker while she's still alive.'

Piers shook his head vehemently. 'I can't allow her to be pulled about and transported and cause her more suffering. I must put her out of her misery. It'll be instantaneous.'

The disgruntled farmer shrugged. 'She's not in all that much pain. She tried to get up at first.'

'Well, of course she would, and it must have been agony.' Piers turned to Lindsay. 'I don't think I'll need your help, but you'd better come and see how this killer works. It's very merciful.'

It was a pitiful sight, but the cow stayed motionless when Piers put the barrel of the hand gun which contained the lethal bolt against its temple and Lindsay fought against a desire to turn away. Piers drew a long breath, pulled the trigger, the bolt went in and it was all over. After making sure, Piers turned to the farmer.

'There will be forms to fill in—I'll do them tomorrow.' As the men came forward to lift the heavy body into the trailer he added, 'We'll be off now.'

As he and Lindsay walked back to his car, he put an arm round her shoulder and said, 'I shouldn't really have let you come—you're upset.'

Grateful for his understanding, she said, 'Do you

know it's the first time I've seen anything like that?'

'Well, it won't be the last. I never like doing it, but it's the kindest way out for many an animal. Sometimes it can be very emotional—someone's horse, for instance. That's really traumatic.'

She looked up at him as he opened the car door. 'I wonder sometimes why I chose to be a vet.'

'Oh, come on. You know it's because you love animals and want to help them.'

'That's true, of course, but——'

'"But me no buts"——' He settled himself into the driving seat. 'What you want, my girl, is a drink.' He grinned at her. 'My place or yours?'

She stifled a laugh. 'Mine, I think. What I'd really like is a strong coffee, then bed.'

His smile broadened. 'This conversation is very suggestive. It's giving me ideas.'

She said sharply, 'I shouldn't think it takes much to do that.'

As he pulled out on to the road, he gave her a quick glance. 'Very much on the defensive, aren't you?'

She shrugged, but said nothing and they drove along in silence until he pulled up outside her flat. He said quietly, 'Do you think I merit a coffee?'

She hesitated, then, hearing the tiredness in his voice, she said, 'Of course. Come along in.'

They sat drinking from mugs in the kitchen and suddenly glancing up at the clock she said, 'Do you realise it's nearly midnight? I've got several operations in the morning.'

He put down his coffee. 'I'll be off in a minute. There's just one thing. My aunt rang me earlier this evening. Apparently Katie isn't coming back with her.

There's a friend—a man—in London she's interested in, much to Aunt Phoebe's dismay. Although I assured her I was pleased for Katie, she doesn't really believe me. So how about joining us for lunch on Sunday?'

'No, thank you, Piers. She doesn't see you very often and I'd feel very much in the way.'

Piers frowned but said no more and when he had gone she reflected on his invitation. It seemed odd, but then he was given to strange behaviour. Of course, being the heir to a title might well make a man wary of matchmakers. In a way he was to be pitied. Love for him overwhelmed her for a while, but then she took a grip on herself. She must tear him from her heart and hope that her love would gradually fade.

Next morning after surgery Lindsay began to operate. Her first patient was the English springer spaniel with the grass seed deep in his ear. His owner said the olive oil had soothed him down, but now he was shaking his head again. He was ready for the anaesthetic and, what with his evident hunger and the irritation in his ear, the poor dog was looking very downcast. An examination was carried out to make sure that he could take the anaesthetic, and once that was given it was a comparatively simple matter to remove the grass seed. Lindsay held it out in the forceps and showed the owner.

'See the shape—like a broad arrow covered with multiple barbs. Sometimes, if it has only just entered the ear, one can get it out by pouring in a generous spoonful of olive oil. Then you have to stand quickly back because the dog immediately shakes his head and very often the seed comes out with the oil.' She laughed. 'It's best to do this in the open, of course.'

'It's a trick worth remembering,' the owner said. 'I'll try it out next time.'

The next patient was a collie with a growth, and its owner, a nervous-looking man, plainly feared the worst. After working swiftly and expertly, Lindsay examined the tumour.

'I feel reasonably sure it's not malignant,' she said, 'but you mustn't take my word for it. I'm going to send it off to the laboratory for investigation. I'll give you the answer as soon as I get it.'

Still trembling, the man said, 'I won't uncross my fingers till then.'

Alison laughed. 'I'd like to know how you're going to cope with crossed fingers for about three days.'

He gazed at her anxiously, then, seeing the amusement in her face, he relaxed.

'You mustn't worry,' Alison said kindly as she led him out, and stayed talking to him for a few minutes. She came back flushed, and laughed at Jessica's obvious curiosity.

'I just gave him a little TLC—tender loving care to you,' she said. 'He's nice. He wanted to make a date with me, but I haven't committed myself.'

'Well, be careful,' Jessica frowned. 'You never know nowadays.'

'Oh, rubbish!' Alison laughed. 'I've seen him before. I know where he lives and some of his friends. My instinct tells me he's OK.'

As Lindsay began to operate on the cats, she pondered on the contrast between the two nurses: Alison, happy-go-lucky, who believed in following her instincts, and Jessica, so wary of danger that she never took chances. Concentrating on her patient, she put

her musing aside until she had finished, but once the
spays were done and she sat down waiting for coffee
the thoughts returned. Into which category would she
put herself? Reluctantly she decided that she was more
like Jessica than Alison, which somehow she found
rather depressing. Suddenly she realised that Alison
had brought Piers' name into the conversation with
Jessica, and her attention was caught in spite of herself.

'That's what Mrs Digby told my mother. His aunt
is coming down either today or tomorrow, so perhaps
we'll see something of her. Do you remember that the
last time she had coffee with us she brought those
luscious pastries? I wonder——?' She broke off.
'Listen—that's Piers' car.' She got up and went to the
window. 'Yes, it's him, and I think——' She nodded.
'Look, Jessica—he's brought his aunt with him.'

CHAPTER NINE

PHOEBE was around sixty, with a good figure and silvery hair. Her only resemblance to Piers lay in her eyes and the smile that lit up her face when Lindsay was introduced.

'Piers is always singing your praises,' she said. 'I do hope you will stay on in the practice, though Piers tells me you haven't yet decided.'

As Piers led her into the office, Lindsay turned to the nurses, who were engaged in opening a box of what proved to be the 'luscious pastries' Alison had described.

A few minutes later they were all sitting at the table with a fresh supply of coffee. The friendly talk was at last brought to an end when Piers looked at his watch.

'We'd better be on our way.' He laughed at his aunt. 'That's if you're able to eat any lunch after those éclairs you've consumed.'

'Oh, you know me, Piers. I've got a good country appetite.' She laughed as she got up and turned to Lindsay. 'Won't you join us? Piers says you can't manage it, but couldn't you try?'

Flushed with embarrassment, Lindsay still shook her head regretfully. 'Honestly—I'm sorry. Thank you very much, all the same.'

'Ah, well—another time, I hope, and I'm sure there will be other times.' Turning, she said goodbye to the nurses and went out, followed by Piers.

As the door closed Alison said, 'Why on earth didn't you go with them?' Curious as usual, she looked puzzled. 'It was obvious she wanted you to.'

Lindsay shrugged and gave the same excuse she had given Piers, but Alison said, 'They may not see each other often, but Piers rings her up a lot. He's told her all about you.'

'Good grief! You never to cease to amaze me, Alison. Your mother and Mrs Digby must be forever discussing Piers' private life.' Half amused and half annoyed, Lindsay stared at her informant, who grinned back at her.

'They're a couple of the biggest gossips I've ever met,' she said.

'So are you.' Jessica frowned at her colleague. 'I think it's awful the way Mrs Digby listens in when Piers is on the phone. How does she manage it? Does she have an extension in another room?'

'Oh, no, she doesn't do that, but she somehow manages to be within earshot.'

'She eavesdrops, you mean,' said Jessica scornfully. 'Someone ought to warn Piers.'

'I suppose they ought.' Alison looked thoughtful. 'It is rather awful when you come to think of it. Mind you, my mother doesn't pass on things to other people. Only to me, of course.' She turned to Lindsay. 'What did you think of Piers' aunt?'

'I liked her. As you said, she's really friendly and kind. She seemed a bit preoccupied when she came in, but after talking to Piers in the office she brightened up considerably.'

'Ah, well! I expect that was because Piers would have told her once and for all that he didn't give a damn about the girl she had hoped he would marry. She probably thought he would be disappointed to hear he'd lost her.'

Once more Jessica and Lindsay listened open-mouthed to Alison's analysis of a situation that was supposedly known only to Piers and his aunt. Lindsay frowned.

'You make me feel uncomfortable, Alison. You're too well-informed. It's awful to discuss other people's private lives. Piers would be furious if he knew.' Still frowning, she went up to her flat, and as she sat eating a light snack she reflected on the impression Piers' aunt had made on her. She had not expected anyone so open and easy to talk to. She was not the possessive type, and it was obvious that she only wanted her nephew's happiness. The invitation had been quite pressing, but Lindsay didn't regret having refused. She couldn't endure too many questions and was afraid of betraying the fact that she was in love with Piers. Apart from the fact that she felt uneasy about the eavesdropping housekeeper, she put all other matters out of her mind and prepared to go back to the surgery and work.

She was alone in the office when Piers walked in.

'I've just taken my aunt to the station.' He paused and gazed at her thoughtfully. 'She was very taken with you and was sorry that you wouldn't have lunch with us.'

Lindsay shrugged. 'Nice of her, but I'm sure you were able to talk more easily than if I had been there.'

'Well, yes. We did talk—quite a lot about this and that. And you, of course.'

'About me? Why on earth——? Oh, I suppose you told her that I had refused the offer of a permanancy here. She seemed to think that I was still undecided.'

He hesitated. 'No, I didn't tell her that. I'm still hoping you'll change your mind. No, don't look like that—you know very well it would be a very foolish thing for you to chuck this chance away. It's a marvellous opportunity for you.'

'It would be if it weren't for your stupid conditions,' she said bitterly, then as a sudden thought struck her she smiled scornfully. 'Of course, I could easily agree to those terms and then, if the situation changed, I could just as easily break them. You wouldn't have a leg to stand on because those conditions would come under the heading of sexual discrimination. You yourself said there would be no need to put those conditions to a man.'

To her surprise, he nodded amiably. 'Well, suppose I waive the conditions?'

Her eyes widened in astonishment. She began to speak, then stopped and began arranging papers on her desk. At last, looking up, she said slowly, 'I'll have to think that over. I didn't expect you to cave in like that.'

His face was grim and as she made for the door he stood in her way.

'Let me pass, Piers. I've got things to do.'

'Ah, yes.' His eyes seemed suddenly to blaze down at her. 'Those mysterious things you always have to do when you want to get out of an uncomfortable situation. Well, I also have things to do and one of them is this!'

Before she could protest, she was in his arms, held so tightly that she was unable to struggle. But although his arms seemed like steel his kiss was soft and so tender that hot tears overwhelmed her. As they flowed down her cheeks he began to kiss them away so lovingly that she thought her heart would break. How could she go on resisting him when she loved him so much that her very bones seemed to turn to water when his lips met hers?

Suddenly he released her and, pulling out a handkerchief, handed it over and stood watching as she wiped her face and tried to control her desperate weeping. As her eyes cleared she looked at him and saw that he looked desolate. He said harshly, 'You've made it plain. You find me repellent. I must be the biggest fool that ever was. I really thought you were beginning to care for me and that all your excuses were because you were afraid of betraying your feelings.'

He paused, looking so stricken that she longed to tell him how wrong he was, but no words came. Instead she turned away in order to control herself and disguise her tears from the nurses when she had to go out of the room.

He said quietly, 'I'll shut the door behind me and keep the girls at bay. Try not to cry any more. I hate myself for making you weep. Please forgive me. I've learnt my lesson.'

In a moment he was gone and she stood motionless. She heard voices and then laughter and thought bitterly, He's able to put on an act for them as though nothing had happened, so his apparent desolation didn't go very deep.

At last the deadly numbness left her and she went to the sink and dashed cold water over her eyes. Suddenly she realised all was quiet in the surgery. Somehow Piers must have enticed the nurses outside, leaving her free to dash up the inner stairs to her flat.

A minute later, from her upstairs window, she saw him explaining something to do with his car. How on earth, she asked herself, could he have managed to get them so interested in such a subject? She shrugged. It was all in character—he could charm any woman, just as he had charmed her. Then, reproaching herself, she acknowledged that that was unfair. He was doing it for her, shielding her from their curiosity. She also must put on an act. Accordingly, she washed her face, and practised smiling until eventually all traces of her breakdown disappeared.

Just in time, as it happened, for suddenly an emergency case arrived. The noise of a car pulling up in the yard drew her to the window again and she saw a man get out holding a large dog in his arms. Piers went forward to help and the nurses led the way into the surgery. Drawing a long breath, Lindsay rushed down the stairs to join them.

The man's face was ashen. 'My own dog—Bruno— I ran him down as I drove out of the garage. I'd no idea he was there. God! It was awful! He's badly hurt—I don't know——' He stopped as Piers helped him to put the German shepherd on to the table and glanced quickly at Lindsay.

She nodded confidently as she set about her examination, but when at last she looked up she could only shake her head.

'I'm afraid it's too late—look.'

There was no doubt at all. One last gasp and the dog lay still. In spite of doing everything possible to revive him, they had no success. At last, as the unfortunate man stood shaking with shock, Jessica quietly put on the kettle. He turned and said wildly, 'No, I don't want tea. I need a proper drink.'

Quickly Piers went into the office and came out with a bottle and a glass. He said, 'I'll drive you home,' and handed him the drink.

Looking down at his dog, the man said harshly, 'Please keep him here for a while. I can't take him back till I've told my wife. She's pregnant and I'll have to get the doctor—in case. Later I'll bury Bruno in the garden.'

When Piers returned, he glanced quickly at the nurses' red eyes and took gratefully the coffee Lindsay handed him. She said, 'We've wrapped him in a large blanket and put him in the other room. How did that poor man cope with his wife?'

'It was awful. He asked me to go in with him. The poor girl went into hysterics. Luckily the doctor arrived just after us and gave her a sedative.'

Lindsay said, 'I've been thinking about the burial of Bruno. Isn't there a new law about that?'

Piers nodded. 'Yes, but it's complicated and personally I think it's utterly stupid. My judgement in this case is that there is no question of infection to cause a health hazard, therefore the owner has the right to do as he wishes.' He sighed. 'Nowadays there is such a multiplicity of new laws that it's becoming almost impossible to obey them in every case.' He paused, then said, 'This kind of incident must be dealt with humanely.'

There was silence for a while, then gradually the atmosphere lightened and the conversation became general. Suddenly, as so often, the telephone rang and Piers picked up the receiver. He said very little, made a note on the pad, then with a short, 'I'll be right over,' he replaced the telephone and picked up his case. 'An accident—a horse box on its side—three racehorses.' He turned to Lindsay. 'It might be a job for two vets—will you come along? It's not far—on the bypass.'

Almost before she had time to take in what had happened, she found herself sitting beside Piers in his Land Rover. He seemed deep in thought, then he said, 'Apparently the driver and two grooms are safely out and unhurt, so let's hope the horses haven't panicked and injured themselves.'

There was no sign of panic when they arrived at the scene. The three men were sitting on the grassy bank for all the world as though they were taking a well-earned rest. As Piers got out of the Land Rover they rose to their feet. The head groom said, 'We haven't attempted to open the door yet. Thought we'd better wait for you.' He paused. 'Three mares in the box— we've just been to the races. They're very valuable. They've quietened down now. We'll have to take it slowly—remove the partitions first. They're pretty well-protected by padded walls inside the box. No expense spared where they're concerned. Do you know——' he grinned wryly '—I got through to Colonel Johnson, the owner, to tell him we'd had this accident and the first thing he said was, "How are the horses?" It was only as an afterthought that he asked, "Any of you hurt?" Typical.'

Piers smiled sympathetically. Then he said, 'Well, when you open up you must try to get head-collars on before you remove the partitions. That way I can administer a light sedative so they'll be less likely to

stand on each other when they get up.' He turned to
Lindsay. 'Will you get three syringes ready, please,
and hand them to me when I'm up there?'

Lindsay looked at the large rear doors lying on their
sides and caught her breath. How on earth were they
going to persuade the horses to clamber out? They
might well damage themselves in the struggle. She
turned away to prepare the syringes, then stood and
watched as the men placed a ramp ready. As the
grooms went to prise open the doors, Piers talked
soothingly to the imprisoned horses, who, surprisingly,
stayed quiet at the sound of his voice. She held her
breath as she saw Piers clamber into the box after
taking the syringes. A few minutes later the first mare
was gently cajoled up to the open doors and led carefully down the ramp, to be followed at intervals by
the other two. They seemed unscathed, but each one
was carefully examined by Piers, who, much to the
groom's relief, pronounced them to be unhurt. He said,
'The Colonel is sending another box to collect them.
It should be here soon.'

Even as he spoke, one of the other men pointed
and Lindsay watched as a horse box pulled up behind
them. Disliking the appearance of the tall, angry-
looking man who got out, she took refuge in Piers'
Land Rover. Ten minutes later he joined her, muttering something under his breath. Aloud he said,
'Pompous old devil. Those grooms are going to get it
in the neck even though the horses aren't hurt.'

He rubbed his leg and she said anxiously, 'Did you
get kicked when you were giving the injections?'

'Just a bit of a knock. I'll rub something on it when
we get back.' He laughed. 'The old-fashioned liniment

I told you about. It was given to me by the man who looked after my father's horse.'

Suddenly interested in his background, Lindsay asked curiously, 'Does your father still ride?'

'No. He gave it up soon after he retired when he had a fall which left him with a groggy leg.'

'What was your father—I mean before he retired?'

Piers laughed. 'He was a rather high-up civil servant. Very dull, but he did something special for the government and that's why they gave him a knighthood.' He paused. 'He himself was quite pleased, but my aunt says he always gets charged more for anything when he gives his name.'

Lindsay laughed. Then, as a sudden thought struck her, she said, 'A knighthood—that's not hereditary, is it?'

He glanced at her quickly. 'Of course not. Did you think it was?'

She shook her head. 'To tell the truth I never gave it any thought, but Alison and Jessica told me once that the reason Mrs Lockwood was after you was because one day you would, as they put it, have a handle to your name.' At the sight of his amusement she went on, 'Fiona, too, was being pushed your way, but she has other plans.'

'Good God! That rather brings me down to size, doesn't it?' His rueful expression made Lindsay smile, and when he added, 'I thought it was me they were after,' she burst out laughing.

He drove in silence for a few minutes then he said, 'It's not really very funny. How could such an ignorant idea have got around?'

He looked so crestfallen that she took pity on him.

'No harm done. After all, you've never misled any-one into thinking you were going to be Sir something or other.'

'My father would have to be a baronet for that,' he said sharply, then, infected by Lindsay's laughter, he began to chuckle. 'Well, this puts me very much on my guard. If any girl looks at me twice in future, thinking I'm going to inherit a title, I'll have to put her straight pretty quickly. Then perhaps she'll no longer be interested in me. And that's a very humbling thought. Puts me properly in my place. When I look back. . .' He shook his head ruefully. 'Well, perhaps I'd better not. What a good job I never proposed marriage. What a let-down that would have been for my ambitious bride.'

There was a touch of bitterness in his voice, and she stayed silent for a while, until he said, 'What are you thinking?'

She shrugged. 'I was thinking that this will make you even more cynical.'

'Certainly it will. It's rather unnerving. I shall never know who really fancies me. Well, it serves me right, I suppose.'

It was too much for Lindsay. Once more she broke into laughter, but almost immediately stopped when Piers said, 'That's better. I'd rather hear your laughter than see your tears. That's something I find hard to take.' He glanced at her quickly. 'There was so much I wanted to say to you, but I realise now that it would only have made matters worse.'

There was a dryness in Lindsay's throat that made it impossible to say anything. In any case, she could find no words to express her feelings, no words to explain to him that he had misinterpreted the whole situation.

These thoughts were still with her when late that night she found she could not sleep. She had driven him away and it was obvious that he would never risk being humiliated again.

Suddenly, just as she was drifting into troubled sleep, she heard a noise outside that made her suddenly alert. Switching on the bedside lamp, she got out of bed and went to the window.

Down in the yard she saw a battered-looking car with a youth standing beside it. Another youth held something in his arms which she guessed must be a small animal. Pulling on a dressing-gown, she pushed up the window. The youths looked up, said something quickly to each other, then called out.

'We've got a sick dog here. Found him in the gutter. Must have been run over.'

All her veterinary instincts took charge, and she called back, 'I'll be right down.'

Closing the window, she looked at her watch. Two a.m. Sighing, she flung on some clothes and before going down the stairs leading into the surgery she took a final look out of the window. There was something suspicious about the youths' behaviour and, careful not to be seen, she gazed at them uneasily. There were four young men in a group talking among themselves, the dog was now back in the car and as they drew near to the surgery window and began peering in she felt a sharp stab of alarm. She stood for a moment wondering what to do. It could be a genuine emergency, but she mustn't take the risk. Picking up the telephone, she tapped out Piers' number and sighed with relief when he answered drowsily. Half apologetically, she told him quickly of her suspicion and instantly he became alert.

'Don't let them in. I'll be right over.'

She waited a few minutes, then, as they began to shout for her, she went to the window.

'You'll have to wait a bit. I'm looking for an injection. I won't be long.'

Watching cautiously, she saw them muttering and gesticulating. All their gestures seemed threatening and, thoroughly alarmed by now, she wondered if she ought to ring the police. Better to look foolish if the incident was genuine than risk Piers getting hurt. She picked up the telephone again. The local police promised her that they would come round immediately and, reassured, she went to the window. Now one youth was drinking from a bottle and the others were prowling round the yard. No one was showing any concern for the dog shut in the car.

Suddenly, headlights blazing, the Land Rover swung into the yard and pulled up beside the battered car. Her heart beating wildly, Lindsay saw the youths walk slowly towards Piers as he leant out of the car window. She could bear it no longer and rushed down the stairs to the surgery. From the window she saw that he was still in the car and heard him say loudly,

'Well, I'm a vet. Where's this dog?'

With increasing alarm she saw him get out holding a gun. But it was only his dart gun—it was merely to frighten them, which it certainly did. There was suddenly a babble of voices as the youths backed away. Two of them went to their car, looked in, then one of them called, 'It's too late. He's dead.' He beckoned to the others and they all scrambled in, in haste, and began to back out of the yard. As the car moved, Lindsay caught sight of the dog, its tail wagging furiously before it was pulled down out of sight. They had nearly reached the exit when suddenly it was blocked by a police car. Drawing a long breath of relief, Lindsay ran out to stand beside Piers, who put an arm round her shoulder.

'Thank God you had the sense to ring me. And the police have been quick. I rang them before I left.'

'I rang them as well.' Lindsay laughed tremulously as she watched the youths being pushed into the police car. 'The dog—there's nothing wrong with it. I saw it wagging its tail.'

He nodded. 'I had a word with the police. Apparently this gang did a doctor's surgery a week ago, saying they had a sick baby in their car.' He looked down at her. 'Lindsay, you're as white as a sheet. Come inside.'

As soon as they entered her flat, he settled her into an armchair and filled the kettle. She tried to laugh.

'Hot, sweet tea—ugh!'

'Best thing for you at the moment.' He sat on the arm of the chair and drew her close. For a few moments she clung to him, grateful for his calm presence, then, when the kettle boiled, he got up to make the tea.

She drank slowly, making a face at the amount of sugar he had put in, then, putting down the empty cup, she said, 'I'm sorry I've been so stupid.'

'Not stupid at all. Thank God you recognised those villains for what they were.' He paused. 'Now you're going straight back to bed and I'll doss down here.'

He went across to the sofa, but she stared at him in consternation.

'You can't stay here! What on earth will people——?'

'No one will know,' he said calmly. 'There's not much of the night left, but I'm not going to leave you here alone.'

'Mrs Digby will know and she's a terrible gossip.'

He grinned reassuringly. 'She won't know a thing. If she's there when I return for breakfast she'll just suppose I was called out to an emergency. Which, of course, I was. Now come along—into your bedroom.' Ignoring her protest, he said grimly, 'If you don't go I'll carry you there and undress you myself—not that you've got much on.'

Suddenly realising that her dressing-gown had fallen open, she fled into her room and shut the door. She heard him call, 'It's nearly morning,' and, falling into bed, she relaxed and was soon in a deep sleep.

She awoke to find that Piers had gone, leaving a note to say that he would do the morning surgery, but would like to see her afterwards to discuss a plan he had in mind. Glancing at her watch, she saw that, if she hurried, she could be in time for surgery after all. It was kind of him to offer to do her work but there was no need—she was fully recovered.

She was only ten minutes late when she arrived, and found that the word had already gone round about the excitement of the night before. Putting on her overall, she went into the examination-room where she found Piers in the middle of a discussion with a nervous client.

'Only a couple of stitches on his torn ear and you can fetch him this evening.' He smiled. 'But he's a real warrier—always fighting and getting damaged. Don't you think it would be better to have him neutered? It would calm him down and stop these nightly battles with the local Romeos.'

When at last the client agreed to allow the operation and the door closed behind him, Piers turned to Lindsay.

'Didn't you read my note?'

She shrugged. 'Yes, and thank you for the offer. But I can take over now.'

He studied her carefully. 'Sure you're OK? No after-effects?'

She laughed. 'None at all. I'm not made of sugar. Honestly, there's no need to be so protective.'

Realising instantly that she had chosen the wrong word, she bit her lip. The nurses glanced at each other and Piers grinned.

'Sugar and spice—that's what they say little girls are made of. More spice than sugar in your case, I think.'

Jessica coughed, Alison stifled a giggle and Lindsay said hurriedly, 'Shall we get on, then? Next patient, please.'

They worked separately and surgery was quickly over, causing Piers to look at his watch.

'Plenty of time for coffee.' He grinned at the nurses. 'Now you shall hear all about the excitement last night. What's more, we'll give you the exact details so there'll be no danger of you getting the facts wrong.' He paused and his mouth twitched. 'I've learnt that a lot of inaccurate gossip has been going the rounds lately. Wonderful how people get little things—titles, for instance—wrong. Whoever heard of a quite ordinary knighthood being passed on to a son?' He stopped and stood looking steadily at the nurses' scarlet faces. 'And, of course, once the error is passed round nobody thinks to question it.' Then, taking pity on his embarrassed listeners, he said, 'Now come on. Let's have that coffee and Lindsay and I will tell you all about last night.'

It didn't take long and the nurses were suitably impressed. Then Piers said, 'This kind of incident made me think about security and I've made a decision about this surgery. It's very vulnerable at present, as is the flat overhead. I've had a word with Jim and this is what we've decided. We're going to transfer the whole surgery to my house. As you know, it's quite large, and if necessary an extension would make it larger. Then I'll get another dog—a German shepherd. That'll make two guard dogs. As regards Lindsay and, later on, any extra assistant we might employ—we'll fix up separate accommodation. What do you think? It'll mean getting planning permission, but I don't anticipate any difficulty there.'

It was obvious that Jessica and Alison thought it a marvellous idea, but later on in the privacy of the office Piers said, 'I grow cold all over when I think of you alone in the surgery last night. God knows what might have happened to you if you had let those young villains in. It doesn't do to dwell on it.' He paused. 'But it's given me an idea and I'd like to know what you think of it. In my house there's plenty of room for a self-contained flat upstairs. It could be made ready in a matter of a week or so. How about it?'

Startled, Lindsay stared at him, then shook her head.

'If you mean for me, then I don't think it's a good idea. Most practices supply accommodation away from the practice if there's no flat over the surgery.'

'Ah, yes, but don't you see? It's often quite late when you finish at night, and in winter it gets dark early. Life nowadays is dangerous enough, and you are very vulnerable alone in that flat. Surely it would be better to live in a house where the security would be very efficient? You would be quite independent.'

She frowned, trying to find an objection, then it came.

'Your housekeeper—she doesn't live in, does she?'

'No. She shares a house in the town with her sister who always fetches her by car.' He raised his eyebrows. 'Aren't you being rather old-fashioned?'

She flushed. 'I suppose I am. Well, I'll think it over. I haven't really committed myself yet to staying on here. Things have happened. . .' She shrugged. 'I might even leave in a week or two.'

Dismay flashed in his eyes for a moment. Then he said smoothly, 'I very much hope you won't.' He paused. 'I've promised to waive all the conditions you objected to—you seemed to agree. I thought it was settled.' He stopped, then added firmly, 'You really must say either yes or no and stop dithering. You've had plenty of time to make up your mind. Surely you know by now?'

It was true. She recognised that she had come to a crossroads in her life. She thought hard for a few moments and suddenly the way ahead became clear. Slowly she began to speak.

CHAPTER TEN

When Lindsay had finished, Piers nodded.

'Agreed. No personal conditions.' He paused. 'Well, a year is a long time and the partnership won't come up till Jim retires next April. If you meet someone before then and want to move a long way from this area, then the whole thing will naturally fall through.'

She thought sadly that no other man would ever replace him in her heart but she said calmly, 'That's understood, but as I very much want to stay in this practice it's not likely that I would allow myself to get involved with anyone who would mean leaving here.'

His eyebrows rose. 'Are you so self-controlled? When one is really in love all caution is thrown to the wind.'

Ah, yes, she thought bitterly, *I* realise that all right. But it takes two to bring about that kind of situation and, in my case, I have to keep my love secret. She said carefully, 'I can't see that happening to me.'

His smile was mocking. 'Want to bet?'

'No,' she said curtly. 'I don't bet on certainties.'

He said nothing, but his eyes held hers for a full minute. Then she could bear it no longer. She began to get up but he waved her down.

'Please, Lindsay. I haven't finished. We must settle this business of accommodation. If you really don't want to live in my house I—well, we, the practice—

will find a suitable flat or small house for you. Meantime, you'll have to put up with my house until we can find what you like.'

She felt a surge of gratitude. 'Thank you very much. I'll do my best to justify your generosity.'

'I'm sure you will,' he said smoothly. 'The only thing——'

He stopped abruptly and, puzzled, she waited in silence. At last she asked, 'What were you going to say?'

He drew a long breath. 'I'm afraid I've made a promise that I'll find impossible to keep.'

Suddenly she was nervous. She thought back to the way he had waived all the conditions to which she had objected but could find no solution. With a slight tremor in her voice she said, 'I don't understand. What promise?'

He looked at her steadily. 'I promised never to treat you other than professionally. I don't think I can stick to that.'

Her heart jumped and for a moment she felt a surge of joy. Then quickly she looked away. He mustn't read it in her eyes. She said calmly, 'What's the alternative?'

'Oh, you must know what I mean. Surely we can have the odd evening out together? Dinner sometimes, or—well, anything that pleases you.'

She sat in silence, longing to say, Yes, of course, but fearful of the danger involved.

He seemed to read her thoughts. 'You're afraid, aren't you?'

To her dismay, she felt her colour rising so, trying to to sound indignant, she said, 'Don't be silly. Why should I be afraid of you?'

'I didn't say you were afraid of me. I think you're afraid of yourself.'

This was so true that she could only take refuge in scorn. 'Don't be absurd. My hesitation was because of difficulties that might occur if we were both off duty at the same time.'

'Oh, that! You know very well that that's no problem. A nurse on duty, mobile phones—even vets are entitled to some social life.'

'Yes, I suppose so.' The mockery in his eyes irritated her. 'But surely we shall see enough of each other every day in our work? It wouldn't be wildly exciting, would it?'

He winced. 'You mean you'd be bored stiff?' Then he laughed wryly. 'You're very hard on me, aren't you? Yet I have the feeling that although you pretend to be an iceberg there are hidden fires in you that could melt away all that cold exterior. I would like to be the one to start that conflagration.'

She swallowed. 'If that's your ambition, then I don't want to go out with you.'

'There you are—that's your trouble. You're afraid of love. You're so inhibited.'

'Love? Who said anything about love?' She looked at him as steadily as she could, then she said impatiently, 'Look—I've had enough of all this crazy analysis of my character.' She paused. 'You're the one who's inhibited, with your ridiculous hang-up about marriage.'

Just as she rose to her feet again, he said suddenly and harshly, 'Sit down, Lindsay. Let's get this clear. You say I've got a hang-up about marriage. Let me tell you that I have very good reason.' He paused and she saw that he had gone very pale. Despite her wish to leave him, she waited as he began to speak. 'Listen to me for a minute, then perhaps you'll understand.'

He drew a long breath. 'My mother left my father, who adored her. Left him quite ruthlessly for another man, who was responsible for the car crash that killed her. She also left me—a child of four. Can you imagine what that did to me? My father did his best, but was too absorbed in his own grief to comfort me. For two years I depended on a nanny for affection, then I was sent to a prep boarding-school where I was extremely unhappy. Things got better when my father's sister came to live with us and look after me. Her marriage had also broken up—her husband was unfaithful and there was a divorce. I grew to love her— I still do—but she couldn't replace my mother. . .

'At thirteen I went on to public school, where I was quite happy. But two of my friends' parents' marriages also broke up and we boys—youths then—became very cynical. That cynicism remains with me. I do not believe in marriage.' He stopped, passed his hand over his forehead then added, 'I do, however, believe in close relationships and I'm convinced that a good one is better than being trapped for life.'

Lindsay said evenly, 'It's not marriage that's at fault. It's people who don't keep the vows they make. Those vows are very serious and beautiful. They contain the whole meaning of love.'

He shook his head impatiently. 'A few words mumbled over you, a few questions and answers— they only make it more difficult when it comes to the usual break-up.' He stopped. 'I can see you're shocked.'

She shook her head slowly. 'I'm not shocked. Lots of people think like you.'

'You don't, though, do you?'

'No; I think you've got it all wrong.' Suddenly she lost patience. 'Oh, let's skip it! I can't think how we got into such an argument. It's a sheer waste of time.'

She stood up and he came round from the desk to open the door for her.

'Not a waste of time at all,' he said smilingly. 'We must discuss it again—perhaps when we have dinner together.' He paused. 'You might even be able to convert me.'

She looked at him scornfully. 'I expect that's a ploy you use in order to persuade some unfortunate girl to enter into what you call a "close relationship" with you.'

He said furiously, 'That's most unfair! You're making me out to be a low kind of seducer.'

She shrugged and retorted, 'If the cap fits. . .' and heard him gasp as she went through the doorway.

For the rest of the morning she tried to put Piers and his ideas out of her mind. In spite of his wish to continue their argument, she knew there was no more to be said. He had joked about the possibility of being converted to her view, but—and here a great wave of uncertainty swept over her—it was far more likely that she would be the one to succumb, because of her love for him.

Pulling herself together, she told herself fiercely that, old-fashioned as she knew her principles were, she would stick to them. What was more, she thought, she certainly must not try to convert him, telling herself that the old adage of 'a man convinced against his will is of the same opinion still' held true. The idea of Piers being dragged unwillingly to the altar made her laugh wryly, and suddenly she felt calm and resigned.

It was not until she went up to her flat for a quick lunch that irritation for a different reason swept over her as she remembered the proposed removal to Piers' house. Dismayed, she wondered how difficult it would be to make him change his mind. Nevertheless, she would try, and when she saw his car sweep into the yard she threw open the window. In answer to her call he looked up and said, 'I was just coming to see you.'

Opening the door to him, she said crossly, 'You know, Piers, I think this move to your house is quite unnecessary. I don't mind going to another flat when you've found one, but I'd rather stay here until then.'

He stood looking round the room. Then he said, 'You've only got your personal things here. They can be easily transferred. I'll sleep here until I've got my house adapted. Meantime Mrs Digby has agreed to sleep in so that you won't be alone, and I'll leave Bruce with you.'

Lindsay drew a long, exasperated breath. 'Piers, you haven't listened. I said I'd stay here until you find accommodation for me. There's no point in my going to live in your house.'

He shrugged. 'Well, you can go to Jim and Denise. They have said you'd be very welcome. How's that?'

She frowned. 'That's very kind of them, but——' she hesitated '—well, I'd feel like a guest.'

'So what's it to be?'

'I want to stay here,' she said firmly. 'It's not likely that there'll be another attempted break-in so soon after the other one. In any case, they've got the gang concerned. By the way, what's happened to them?'

'They've been remanded in custody.' Piers smiled grimly. 'The magistrates round here are pretty tough. None of that patting on the back and saying it's all their mother's fault.'

She laughed. 'Well, there you are. Come on, Piers— let me stay here.'

'Sorry.' He shook his head. 'It's not on. Now that I've seen the risk I can't possibly let you sleep here alone. Of course——' he grinned '—I could always move in with you. How about that?'

'No, thanks. That's a risk I'm not prepared to take.' She managed a laugh, but her heart jumped erratically. 'I suppose I'll have to give in and go to your house, but it's very much against my will.' She frowned. 'What's more, I'm not terribly keen on Mrs Digby.'

'It won't be for long. She'll do anything you want. Cook your meals or leave you to cater for yourself— just as you like.'

'I prefer to be independent.' She sighed as she gazed round the room. 'I suppose I'd better start to pack.'

'Have you had any lunch?'

She hesitated, and he added, 'No need to say. Nor have I. So how about sandwiches and coffee for two?'

They ate in silence, but every now and then Lindsay frowned. Suddenly she said, 'Piers, have you thought that moving the surgery might very well be harmful to the practice? Your house is almost out of the town, whereas you have a marvellous central position here. Clients who haven't got cars won't necessarily want to make the journey.'

He nodded in agreement. 'Our minds must be working on the same lines. I'm also beginning to doubt the wisdom of transferring the surgery. How would it be if I—that is, we—engaged a male assistant to share the large-animal work with me? After all, Jim will have to be replaced. The new man could live here in this flat with a guard dog. It would help with the general workload as well. As it is, we don't really get enough time off.' He looked at her steadily. 'Going out together, for example.'

She flushed. 'That's not really relevant, but the rest makes sense. The practice must expand—all practices do, if they don't want to go under. You—we—might eventually get another woman vet to share the small-animal work.'

He looked pleased. 'A good idea. You'll make an excellent partner.'

She smiled wryly. 'Just so long as I agree with you, is that it?'

'No, of course not. But you see ahead. A valuable asset.'

'Well, it's a well-known fact that women have more foresight than men.'

His eyebrows rose. 'So can you see the future where we're concerned? A good professional partnership, yes—even I can see that—but what kind of personal relationship shall we have?'

'Don't be stupid. I'm not a fortune-teller.' She spoke sharply, but her eyes avoided his questioning look. 'I see no reason why it should be anything other than professional.'

'That's very discouraging to me. I'll tell you what I hope for.' He paused, then said softly, 'Look at me, Lindsay. Come on—look me straight in the eye. Do you care for me at all?'

Colour flooded into her face and she felt her knees shaking as she stared at him speechlessly. Even in her condition of shock, she saw that he had gone very pale and his lips were pressed together as though to stop them trembling. Silence hung between them for a full minute, then he spoke again.

'Perhaps that's not a fair question. It might be better if I told you how I feel about you.' He hesitated and before he could continue she found her voice.

'I don't want to know.' She got up quickly and made for the door, but he was there first. Barring her way, he took her by the shoulders and held her tightly, in spite of her immediate resistance. Bending his head, he was about to kiss her when she said fiercely, 'If you do that, Piers, it's all over with the partnership.'

He drew back slowly and as his grip relaxed she freed herself, opened the door and went down to the surgery. The nurses had gone and she was just going into the recovery-room when she heard a sound in the waiting-room. A dog was whining and a woman's voice was trying to soothe it. Immediately she opened the door a fat little mongrel cowered back. Its owner said sharply, 'Fred doesn't like this place. He remembers his last injection. I brought him along early so that he wouldn't have to wait, but I've been here ages. He needs his booster injection and he knows it, I'm sure.'

Putting aside all the confusion in her mind caused by Piers, Lindsay concentrated on her patient. Before giving the injection, she gave the dog a thorough examination, then, after giving him the booster so swiftly and skilfully that the little dog hardly noticed, she said, 'You know your Fred is much too fat. He really must lose weight if he's to live a healthy life.'

After a few questions about the dog's lifestyle his owner had to be persuaded to put him on a special diet to bring his weight down and restore his energy. It was difficult to convince the client, but at last, by dint of explaining the consequences of over-feeding, she agreed to do as suggested, then spoilt everything by promising Fred a 'sweetie' for having been such a good boy.

Lindsay sighed heavily, realising that in this case her advice was wasted, then looked at her watch. Nearly an hour to go before evening surgery, so after seeing off the client she went into the recovery-room to look at the patients due to be returned to their owners.

Suddenly she realised that Piers had followed her and, annoyed, she turned to protest, when the telephone rang. Piers got to it first and she stood by, waiting in case the call was for her. When she realised he was talking to his aunt, she began to move away, but to her surprise he signalled her to stay. Puzzled, she listened, and suddenly he burst out laughing.

'My dear Phoebe, of course I'll do my best, but I doubt if I'll succeed. Anyhow I'll let you know.'

Replacing the receiver, he turned. 'I thought she might want to speak to you, but she's left it to me to issue the invitation. She will be having her sixtieth birthday at the weekend and she's throwing a party. I shall go, of course, and she would like you to come with me.'

'Me? Good heavens! She hardly knows me. I couldn't possibly——'

'Oh, yes. You must. She'll be disappointed. I'll make arrangements with our neighbours—the vets over at Nitton. Don't worry about that.'

Lindsay frowned. 'It's very kind of her, but it's really out of the question.' She paused and looked at him suspiciously. 'Are you sure she really asked me or is it just your idea?'

He shrugged. 'If you don't believe me you can ask her personally. Here's her number.'

'That's ridiculous! How can I do that? But, as I said, she hardly knows me.'

'Ah!' Piers grinned. 'My aunt makes her mind up quickly.' He paused, hesitated, then, his mouth twitching at the corner, he said, 'She also has what you call a "hang-up", only it's the opposite of mine. She wants to get me married and, having met you, she's convinced that, at last, she's found the girl for me.'

'Good grief!' Lindsay's face flamed, then she burst out laughing. 'Well, you'll have to tell her that she's on the wrong track, won't you?' She gazed at him incredulously. 'Doesn't she know your opinion of marriage?'

'Oh, yes. That's why she's so concerned. In spite of all my protestations and her own experience, she still believes I won't be happy until I'm hitched up.'

'And yet you said you'd try to try to persuade me to go. I heard you myself. Piers, I don't think I'll ever understand you. Or——' she paused '—that I even want to. You seem to be playing a very deep game.'

He took a step forward and once more he took her by the shoulders and looked deeply into her eyes. Unresisting, she stood very still, trying not to give way to her longing for his arms to go round her. Then he said slowly, 'Lindsay, I won't pretend any more. Listen.' He drew a long breath. 'Do you know? Haven't you guessed? I love you. Love you with all my heart. I know you're the only girl for me. But I haven't the faintest idea about your feelings for me. This I must know.' His grip tightened. 'I want you so much.'

It was such a shock that she felt almost faint and for a few moments his last words didn't register. Then, at last, they echoed in her mind and her breath came fast. He wanted her just as she wanted him, and she was only held back by what he called her inhibitions. Then suddenly she remembered what he had said on another occasion about affairs that inevitably broke up and her heart sank. Oh, yes, she loved him, but still she couldn't give herself to him in a relationship that was not likely to be permanent. She shut her eyes for a moment, unable to stand the way he was watching her, then, opening them, she returned his searching gaze.

She said simply, 'Yes, Piers. I do love you. I have for a long time. But——'

He swept her into his arms so fiercely that she cried out, but he said, 'Oh, my darling! My darling!' Then she felt his lips on hers and she no longer held back and as his kiss became more passionate she knew she was lost.

When at last they drew apart, she put her hand up to his cheek and stroked it gently, saying quietly, 'I know my love for you will last, but what about yours? Is this going to be just another affair for you?'

He released her and gazed down at her almost accusingly. For a moment she thought she had angered him, but almost immediately he opened his arms again and she went into them, hiding her face against his chest while he buried his face in her hair. He said brokenly,

'How can you doubt me? You've got good reason, I know, but this *is* the deep love you told me about. The love that will last for always. Will you give me the chance to prove it?'

'Yes, oh, yes.'

Her reply was whispered, but he heard and covered her face with kisses, murmuring words of love until she thought her heart would burst. Then, suddenly, the telephone rang and he exclaimed ruefully, 'Damn and blast! This will be typical of our life together, I suppose.' With one arm still round her, he picked up the receiver and listened impatiently. 'OK,' he said. 'I'll be right over.' Reluctantly he let her go. 'A bad calving case—I'll have to go. Darling Lindsay, how can I leave you?'

She watched him go, then sat down almost in a daze.

His kisses still burning her lips, she looked into her mind. She had made her decision and no matter what the future held she knew she would never regret it. She had abandoned her principles, but now they seemed of no account. 'Piers, Piers,' she murmured, 'I'll love you forever and nothing else matters.'

She got through evening surgery in that same daze, although she did her best to hide her inner glow from the nurses' curious glances. She felt that she was walking on air and never had she found it so difficult to concentrate on her patients. Luckily none of them presented any problems, but it was with a huge sigh of relief that she heard the door close behind the last client. Turning, she saw the nurses gazing at her in open curiosity, and Alison said, 'You look as though someone's left you a fortune. Have you had some good news?'

Lindsay tried to speak calmly. 'Well, not exactly that kind of news but—well, I'll tell you more another time. At the moment I must get on with packing my things up. Piers——' the very moment she said his name she could feel her face burn and hurriedly turned away '—Piers will be sleeping here tonight and I have to go to his house until he can get some accommodation fixed up for me.'

Satisfied with her explanation, they went away and she went up to her flat and tried to concentrate on gathering her things together. Then suddenly, with a jumping heart, she thought of the coming night. What was in his mind? Would their love be consummated here in her flat? A wave of panic swept over her and she began to pace her room until at last she was brought up abruptly by the sound of his car in the yard. She heard him running up the stairs then in a moment she was in his arms again and her fears vanished.

At last he let her go, took a quick glance round the room and said, 'Darling, I see you've got everything ready. Let me take these cases and we'll have dinner at my house. I've told Mrs Digby she can have the evening off and that she needn't come back till late, just so that you won't be alone in the house tonight.'

For a moment she felt chilled. He sounded so matter-of-fact. What was he planning? He saw her hesitation and looked puzzled.

'What's wrong? You haven't changed your mind, have you? The arrangement still stands, doesn't it? I'll sleep here and I'll know you're safe in my house. That's all right, isn't it?'

She smiled tremulously. 'Of course, although I'm

not looking forward to being spied on by Mrs Digby. I'm afraid she'll sense that I—that we. . .'

Her voice trailed away as he took her in his arms once more.

'You're not to worry about anything, my darling. Come along now and we'll have a wonderful celebration dinner together.'

As she sat on the terrace watching Piers open a bottle of champagne, her glow of happiness returned. Nothing mattered now. She had found her love returned in full measure and there were no more decisions to be made. Looking around, she felt that all of nature was sharing her joy. The May evening was warm and scented with flowers, while birdsong supplied music that echoed in her heart. Piers lifted his glass to her.

'To you, my darling, and our life together.' He paused. 'I can scarcely believe my luck.' Then he chuckled. 'I'm looking forward to seeing my aunt's face when I introduce you as my fiancée.'

Lindsay's hand shook as she put down her glass. 'What—what did you say?'

'I said my fiancée—what's wrong with that?'

She was trembling now and she felt the colour draining from her face. Looking at him mutely, incredulously, Lindsay opened her mouth to speak, then shook her head as no words came.

'Lindsay, what is it? What have I said?' Alarmed, he reached across the table and grasped her hand. 'You're shaking! What's happened? Oh, God! Don't say you've changed your mind.'

She saw the fear in his eyes and drew a long breath. 'Nothing is wrong. It's just that——' It was difficult to find the right words but at last she said, 'I thought you only wanted—well, a relationship.'

He gasped. 'A relationship? And you were going along with that? Sacrificing all your principles for me! My darling—is that so?'

She nodded mutely and suddenly his eyes were full of tenderness. He said very slowly, 'Now I know that you really love me. And you make me ashamed. I've been an arrogant fool. Listen, my beautiful darling. I've never known real love till now and with that revelation I realise that marriage with you will be the nearest thing to heaven I'll ever get in this life.' He paused. 'How does it go? "To have and to hold. . . for richer for poorer, in sickness and in health, to love and to cherish, till death us do part".'

Tears of joy were filling her eyes and he got up, came round to her and wiped them tenderly away with his handkerchief. Then he picked up her glass, took a sip and put it to her lips. 'Share it with me, just as we'll share everything in future.'

Dusk had fallen when at last they went indoors and the scented evening seemed to fill the house with love and the promise of happiness that would always be deep and true.

MILLS & BOON

are proud to present...

A set of warm, involving romances in which you can meet some fascinating members of our heroes' and heroines' families. Published each month in the Romance series.

Look out for "Make-Believe Family" by Elizabeth Duke in August 1995.

Family Ties: Romances that take the family to heart.